Jakey's Fork
A River's Journey

Excerpts in Chapter 2, "Behemoths," are borrowed from "My Road to Hell," a delightful chapter in Ann Patchett's collection, *This Is the Story of a Happy Marriage* (2013). I am grateful to the author for her kind permission to use her words.

Published by Pepys2000 Writing   *pepys2000.blogspot.com*

ISBN: 9 78099 848203
Library of Congress Control Number: 2018901326
Printed in the United States of America

Design & Layout by Rod Burton
Cover Photo by Richard Little

Jakey's Fork
A River's Journey

Richard Little

Bellingham, Washington

Table of Contents

Let us go then, you and I,
When the evening is spread out against the sky …
Let us go and make our visit.
>—T. S. Eliot, *The Love Song of J. Alfred Prufrock*

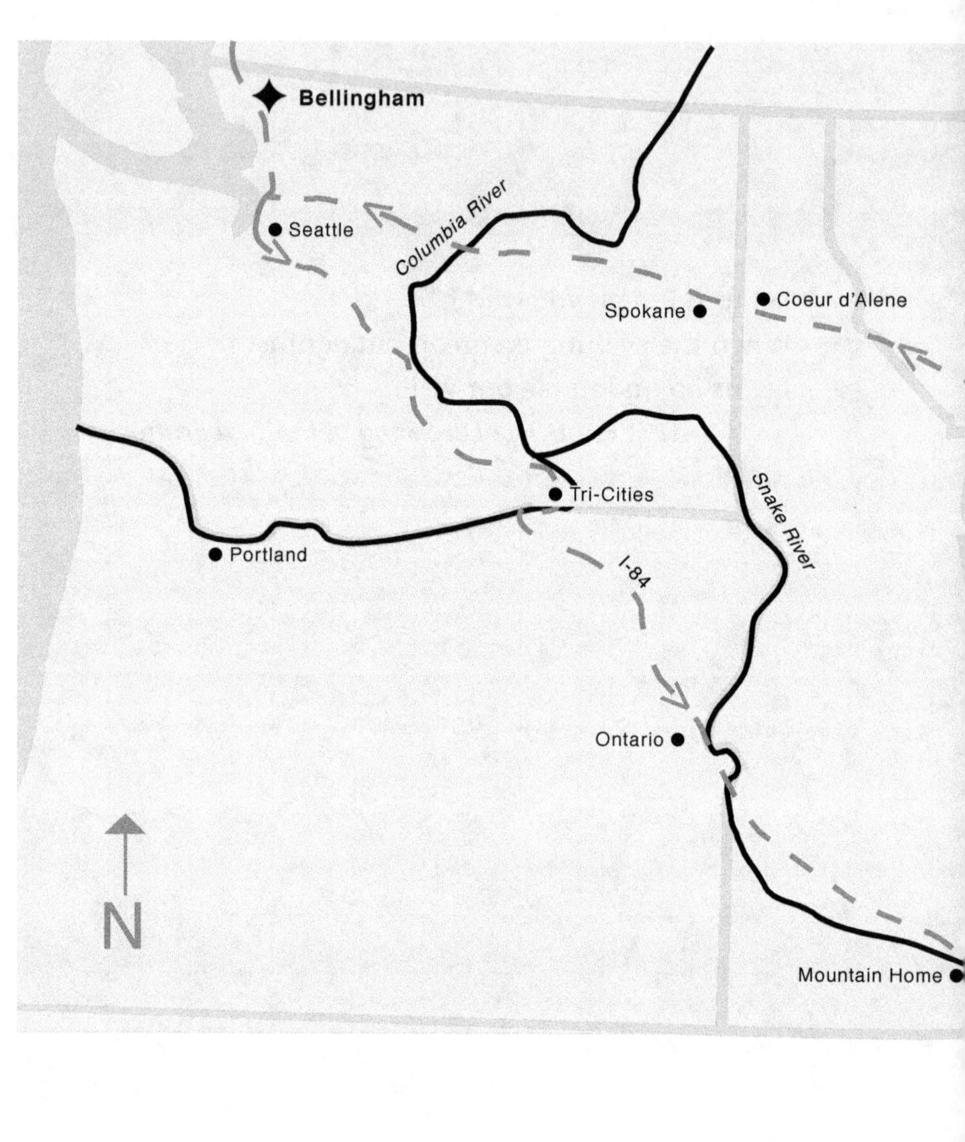

Bellingham
Seattle
Columbia River
Spokane
Coeur d'Alene
Tri-Cities
Snake River
Portland
I-84
Ontario
Mountain Home
N

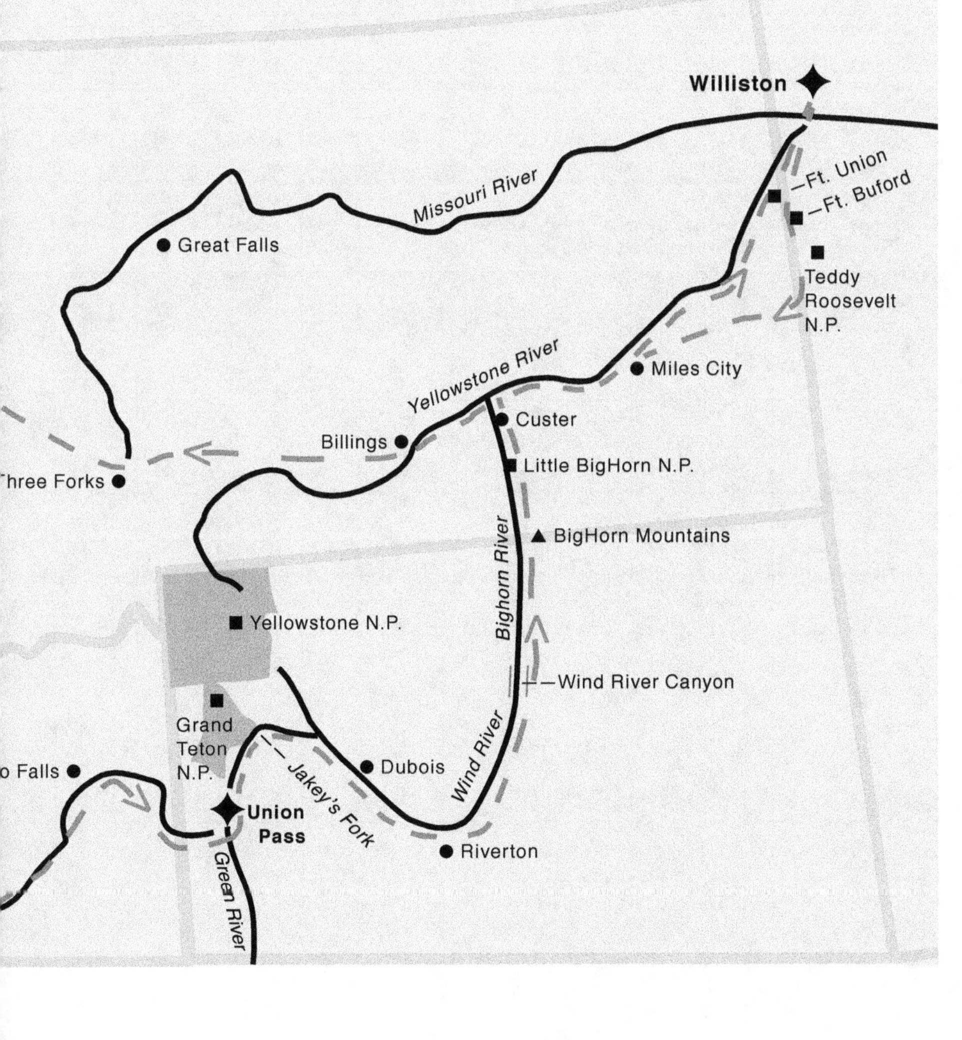

Williston
Missouri River
Great Falls
Ft. Union
Ft. Buford
Teddy Roosevelt N.P.
Yellowstone River
Miles City
Three Forks
Billings
Custer
Little BigHorn N.P.
BigHorn Mountains
Bighorn River
Wind River Canyon
Yellowstone N.P.
Wind River
Grand Teton N.P.
Jakey's Fork
Dubois
o Falls
Union Pass
Green River
Riverton

Author's Note
"Fred Nietzsche Tours"

Frederick Nietzsche (1844–1900) is perhaps the last person one would seek out for travel advice before setting off on vacation. Sort of like dropping into "Marquis de Sade Dentistry" about a toothache.

It turns out, however, that before Nietzsche penned the page-turners for which we popped NoDoz in college, *Thus Spoke Zarathustra* and *Beyond Good and Evil*, that before he let the world know that God was dead, and while he doodled away on *The Birth of Tragedy*, Herr Fred wrote an essay in 1872 called "On the Uses and Disadvantages of History for Life." According to Alain de Botton's excellent *The Art of Travel*, Nietzsche argued that collecting facts in a quasi-scientific way was a sterile pursuit. The real challenge should be to use facts to enhance *life*. Quoting Goethe, he said, "I hate everything that merely instructs me without augmenting or directly invigorating my activity."

Nietzsche advised folks not to collect a hundred plant species or count the stones in the Piazza San Marco, but to ponder cultures "which in the past [were] able to expand the concept 'man' and make it more beautiful." In that way, a traveler would have "the happiness of knowing that he is not wholly accidental or arbitrary but grown out of a past as its heir, flower and fruit..."

This idea resonates with me, not for the high art of existentialist philosophy, but rather for an "expanded" search for places to explore. To wit, not learning the precise depth in feet of the Grand Canyon but instead considering how John Wesley Powell might have *felt* rounding a bend and seeing not rapids ahead but open water. How were the bare facts of his journey *enhanced* as he managed, rowing with his one good arm, to conquer the mighty Colorado? Not so much how long Sandro Botticelli took to paint one of his exquisite *Madonnas*. Rather, while he dabbed away at his canvas next to a row of messy paint pots by his easel, what might have gone through his head as he decided on just the right touch for Mary's cheek? What thoughts might have momentarily distracted him while gazing out the studio window in Medici Florence?

My hope is that road trips, foreign and domestic, will be journeys where I'll find the *sense* of a place, not just the place. Of course, it's valuable to do research, to learn what the books say about a destination. But when there in person, I'll try to *under*-intellectualize it, to sit, look, listen … and absorb. How does the history or geography or geology feel? What are the legacies we see in front of us? What might be ours?

Don't be misled, however. No, I can't quite picture the otherwise dour Deutschlander, smiling and sipping schnapps on a cruise up the Rhine, nor envision him leading choruses of "Der fröhliche Wanderer" on weekend treks into the Black Forest. But I will shamelessly use that reference to sneak in the theme of the stories that follow in this collection, namely rivers.

Prologue

Union Pass, Wyoming

There is no other place like it in the country.

Standing on top of the world beneath an impossibly blue sky in the Wind River Range in Wyoming, my wife Cherie and I let it sink in. At Union Pass, 9,212 feet above sea level, a person with a strong arm and good aim could throw a rock in each of three directions, and each missile would splash down in a stream, a tributary of one of the three major river systems in the West: The Columbia, the Colorado, and the Mississippi-Missouri. Water from one large meadow in the Rockies, running to three points of the compass? How does that happen?

Union Pass was known to mountain men and trappers who explored the valley of the Wind River in the early 1800s—John Colter, Jim Bridger, and others. They used it as a route through the Rockies, following the paths of the Native American tribes—Shoshone, Arapaho, Sioux, Blackfoot, and Cheyenne—that for many centuries knew of Union Pass and its significance. They called it the "Land of Many Rivers."

Chilly and zipped up in jackets despite the heat in the valley below, we had the place to ourselves. To the south, Union Peak rose another twenty-three hundred feet, and mountain crests sketched the horizon in every direction. The big sky spread out forever as we stood and contemplated the significance of the place and our insignificant presence within it.

From this unique spot on the continent, we chose one of the three fledgling watercourses, a little creek called Jakey's Fork, and followed where it led—out of the meadow, through forests and past fields, past valleys and towns—to learn about its journey. Beginning high above the tree line, we planned to track the small stream from its trickle seeping out of a marshy pond until hundreds of miles later its successor would meet a massive river of history, the mighty Missouri. A cupful of the clear water running past our feet would one day, amazingly, find the Mississippi and then the Gulf of Mexico.

I've enjoyed a lifelong fascination with rivers. Streams, creeks, rivers—they are the why of this adventure. My dad and I used to camp along the Carson River in the Sierra Nevadas of California. He wanted to teach me how to fish; I was content to watch the water race by. Also back in the day, a childhood friend and I spent hours trying to snag crawdads out of the creek behind my grandmother's cabin in the Santa Cruz Mountains. Our wrinkled and numb fingers got pinched by the angry critters before they scooted back to safety in the rocks.

Our house where I grew up in Sacramento was about a half mile from the American River. Lush rows of green hops separated our street from a levee. I have teenage memories of escaping into the tangle of weeping willows and riparian brush along the river, the experience enhanced by the company of a pretty neighbor girl who lived down the street. We'd sit and talk. (That's all! She already had a boyfriend, sad to say.) The landscape buzzed while the full, brown river rolled by. Formative stuff.

While I was still in high school, my dad gave me a copy of *Across the Wide Missouri*, for which the great Bernard DeVoto won the Pulitzer Prize for History in 1948. Tales of the opening and exploration of the American West captivated me. I still have the book.

Rivers, their legacies—their present and past, their blue traceries across maps, their ancestral power to shape the planet, and their biological and ecological importance—are reasons enough to be enchanted. Rivers as well are paths that carried history: They marked trade routes and migrations. Think Nile, Tigris and Euphrates, Danube, and Yangtze.

Images and metaphors of rivers have infused our culture for millennia. In the sixth century BCE, the philosopher Heraclitus famously dipped his foot in a river, then declared it a different river when he did it again a moment later. The only constant is change, he taught.

Today, the Wild and Scenic Rivers Act is a landmark to the importance of preserving unaltered rivers. Sponsored by a fine senator from Idaho, Frank Church, and signed by President Lyndon Johnson in 1968, the act now saves for posterity all or part of nearly thirteen thousand rivers.

Wallace Stegner, chronicler par excellence of the American West, had this to say about a trip down the San Juan River, a tributary of the Colorado:

> I gave my heart to the mountains the minute I
> stood beside this river with its spray in my face
> and watched it thunder into foam, smooth to
> green glass over sunken rocks, shatter to foam
> again. I was fascinated by how it sped by and
> yet was always there; its roar shook both the
> earth and me.

An image such as this is what Virginia Woolf might have dubbed a "moment of being."

Thus it was that Cherie and I set off eastward out of the Rocky Mountains in the early summer of 2016. With only a few specific destinations in mind, we'd take the time to pull over, unpack lunch, and sit beside a simple, moving body of water—to watch persistent, wet molecules defy river rocks and conquer sandbars. We'd let ourselves be quiet and simply stare at a silken current sliding between million-year-old boulders.

As a specific quest, we'd seek out confluences, places where each creek joined a larger sibling. We would take side roads and dirt roads, perhaps stumble through bulrushes and cattails or mud and horsetails, if necessary, to mark the physical spot where one river joined another. As on other road trips, we'd lap up the history, stories, and people we'd find along the way.

No surprise, then, that we found more than rivers. To wit, wonderful slices of Americana: Watering holes and Winnebagos, jet-setting wine aficionados and Butch Cassidy, and George Armstrong Custer, Sitting Bull, and Theodore Roosevelt. Also dinosaurs.

"Let us go then, you and I ..."

1

Jakey's Fork

Higher-than-normal temps were the rule after we crossed the Cascade Mountains from our northwest corner of the Continental US, including a freaky-high 107 degrees when we stopped for gas in south-central Washington. Readings in the nineties followed us much of the way on this trip across the Rockies and beyond.

The highway followed the old Oregon Trail—up notoriously steep Cabbage Hill out of Pendleton, Oregon, on the diagonal past La Grande and Baker City, and then into Idaho at Ontario. We stayed the first night in Mountain Home. Whatever the source of that town's name—and accounts vary—the Chamber of Commerce preferred it to "Rattlesnake Station," site of the onetime stagecoach stop and original post office nearby.

We slept well after eleven hours on the road. Breakfast, served at a convenient restaurant next door, was a welcome variation from the usual expanded-motel-lobby-cum-cereal-and-steam-table-scrambled-eggs fare. Back to the room, the late-morning walk across the parking lot was h-o-t.

We lugged luggage out to the car, which I managed to locate by beeping the key fob (disdaining Cherie's pointing). A frequent gap in my synapses has to do with not recalling where I left the car—parking lot, side street, field. Plus, our spiffy modern vehicle is indistinguishable from other late-model sedans on the road but for the emblem on the grill.

I set the suitcases down. Black as polished onyx, the car had absorbed every therm of heat the prairie sun had thrown at it since dawn. I opened the door, stepped back, and waited for the gusts of super-heated air to escape. Inside, the seat cushions felt like upholstered hot plates. The steering wheel was like the business end of a fireplace poker. Air-conditioning fought the good fight and had prevailed by the time I paid for the room.

The highway continued on the Oregon Trail's sweeping curve through southern Idaho until Pocatello. From there our route angled northeast to Idaho Falls before entering Wyoming south of the Tetons.

Rivers always run brimful the first weeks of June, all the more when atypical heat in the mountains speeds up the snowpack melt. South of the Grand Tetons near Jackson, Wyoming, we met the west-flowing Snake River, full and racing along, creased with creamy-white wavelets across its width from bank to bank. Leaving the Grand Tetons, we drove east and started to gain serious elevation. The highway continued to climb until we crossed the Continental Divide at Togwotee Pass (pronounced "toe-ga-tee") at 9,584 feet. From there, high in the Absaroka Range of the Rocky Mountains, the Wind River began its descent down the eastern side of the Divide.

We caught glimpses of the eponymous river as it grew in volume, mile by mile, running along the foot of the Wind River Range to our right. The water was a ruddier brown than its sister, the Snake, due to iron in the soil that the Wind pulls from the mountains. It still ran red brown when, just south of the town of Dubois, it was fed by Jakey's Fork, the starting place for our expedition. Up a winding dirt road off the main highway was our goal, Union Pass, the birthplace of three rivers.

The day was clear, and the air, mountain fresh. In a broad meadow, instructive signs pointed the way. A granite marker directed us to tiny Fish Creek. That newborn watercourse headed off westward through fields scattered with lupine, then down through sagebrush valleys, conifer forests, and aspen groves. Eventually, it descends to the Gros Ventre River, which in turn joins the Snake River south of Jackson Hole. The Snake, after negotiating Hells Canyon, joins the Columbia River in southeast Washington State, which in turn empties into the Pacific Ocean.

Only a few thousand feet away from Fish Creek, back on the east side of an unnoticeable Continental Divide, little Wagon Creek flowed out of a marshy pond. It would soon join the Green River, which runs south through Wyoming and all of the state of Utah before connecting with the Colorado River far away in Canyonlands National Park. From there, the Colorado carves its famous course through the Grand Canyon, thence on to the Gulf of California. (Note: The Colorado could have, or should have, been called the Green River, which actually travels a longer distance. In 1921, an intense lobbying effort by the state of Colorado won out.)

Lastly, we stood next to Jakey's Fork, the waterway we'd chosen to follow, named for J. K. Moore, the brother of one Charlie Moore, who founded the CM Ranch, one of the oldest ranches in Wyoming. From Union Pass, Jakey's Fork falls two thousand feet, running eastward before rushing into the Wind River. The Wind flows seventy miles south to—appropriately— Riverton, Wyoming, before pirouetting to the north. After negotiating Wind River Canyon, the river emerges, renamed the Bighorn. The Bighorn continues until it joins the Yellowstone, which goes on to the Missouri, and thence down the Mississippi to New Orleans. The Missouri-Mississippi waterway, at 3,700 miles, is the fourth-longest river system in the world.

Jakey's Fork, then, sent us on our way—to geology, geography, and Western legacies.

How could we resist spending the night at a place called "Jakey's Fork Homestead Bed & Breakfast"? On the outskirts of Dubois, Wyoming, just upstream from where Jakey's Fork joins the Wind River, Carolyn Gillette's bed-and-breakfast is a comfortable, restored bunkhouse where a local boy, Butch Cassidy, whiled away Christmas in 1889. Delightful proprietor Carolyn has lived in the upper Wind River valley for thirty years.

"Du-boyce" please, never "Du-bwah," as it was originally pronounced. A senator from Idaho by that name, sporting the Frenchified pronunciation, sat on the Congressional Postal Committee, the responsibilities of which included naming newly formed cities. The countrified name has stuck.

Like many a resident, Carolyn happened on the charming area and simply decided to stay. Minimal precipitation and summer temperatures that average in the high seventies and low eighties have beckoned to about a thousand permanent residents so far, starting well before 1914 when the town was officially founded. We could see why. Dubois lured us in, and we stuck around for four days and nights.

Carolyn Gillette's rustic restoration was perfect, no longer containing the rudimentary bunk beds, straw mattresses, and instructions to leave your boots at the door. Inside the white, weathered log cabin was an old-fashioned stove, a porcelain farmhouse sink, fully stocked china cupboards, an easy chair from a past century, a claw-foot bathtub, a canopy bed, period knickknacks, and book shelves beneath tied-back calico curtains. The front porch and bench overlooked Jakey's Fork as it sped along. A chalkboard sign read, WELCOME DICK AND CHERIE. We slept like proverbial logs. In the morning, Carolyn treated us to a full-on Rocky Mountain breakfast—scrambled eggs, rashers of bacon, sourdough toast, currant jelly from a blue ceramic jam pot, chunky fried potatoes accented by flakes of mild poblano peppers, and refills of campfire coffee. She refused our offer to clean up before setting off for her day job at what she called a "b, b and b"—as in "bed, bath, and beyond," an assisted living facility up the road.

Butch Cassidy was nowhere around. No surprise, because mystery still surrounds his final days and burial. Robert Leroy Parker, born in 1866, is remembered around town as a rancher and a friendly neighbor. Nicknamed "Butch" as a young man, he later borrowed a surname from a mentor, Mike Cassidy (whose name was also an alias), a cattle rustler. A quick learner,

Butch was arrested for shoplifting at fourteen. He was acquitted because, it is said, he'd left a note apologizing for the theft. He turned to crime, as everyone knows, but held good to his promise to never thereafter rob a local bank.

Butch Cassidy departed from the straight and narrow in earnest in June, 1889, when he robbed a bank in Telluride, Colorado, then fled with his compatriots to Robbers Roost, a well-known hideout. He returned to Dubois and used the loot to buy a spread, but ranching was just a front. He went on thieving because, as bank robber Willie Sutton famously said, "That's where the money is." Whether on the lam or otherwise, Butch Cassidy spent Christmas 1889 at home, relaxing and enjoying good company at the Jakey's Fork bunkhouse.

In 1894, Butch was arrested for stealing horses and allegedly running a protection racket. He went to prison for eighteen months, but by 1896 was back to a life of crime. He and the "Wild Bunch" eventually attracted Harry Longabaugh, the Sundance Kid. Their colorful and legendary exploits followed— train robberies, bank holdups—eventually continuing in South America after the duo fled the United States.

The two outlaws probably died in a standoff in Bolivia in 1908. Holed up and surrounded by soldiers, a gunfight ensued. Butch reportedly shot a critically wounded Sundance to put him out of his misery, but their remains were never officially identified. There were later rumors that Butch had escaped South America, undergone facial-reconstruction surgery, and moved back to the US, living until the 1920s.

Unlike the fate of Butch and Sundance, there is no mystery about the source of many a road-trip anecdote, namely, the places where Cherie and I ate. Overheard conversations are fertile ground. At dinner in a restaurant one evening in the heart of cattle ranching and hunting country, we heard this from one table away:

"Do you have anything vegetarian?"

Patient Server: "Uh, fish and chicken."

Moderately Annoyed Customer: "Well, salad?"

PS: "Yes, of course."

MAC: "What kind of dressing do you have?"

PS: "French, blue cheese, and ten hundred island dressing."

MAC (momentarily confused): "I'll have the blue cheese. And red wine, please."

A bottle of chilled red wine was brought, fresh out of the refrigerator, along with two frosted glasses.

MAC (after considering options): "Uh, ma'am, we'd at least like nonfrosted glasses."

PS: "We could nuke them for you."

We wondered how long this pair of citified tourists would stay in Dubois. Maybe they would find a vintner somewhere else, say, Napa. By contrast, we stuck around and ate well.

We had breakfast every day at the Cowboy Café, a crowded sausage-bacon-eggs-pancakes kind of place, with morning coffee strong enough to float a hammer and a savvy waitress right out of Central Casting. Half-glasses perched on her nose and a flowery calico apron draped across her substantial frame, the stern look on her face broke into a smile like sun out from behind a cloud when we took a seat. With the casual aplomb of a toreador finessing a bull, she delivered an order to a table of cowboy-hatted buckos—two plates in one hand and an astonishing four fanned out in the other, bacon still sizzling. One of the old boys asked, "Did you forget the coffee?"

"I'll be back to spill you some, pronto," she replied.

After breakfast, we wandered across the unbusy street and found a by-God soda fountain with the standard lineup of vinyl-topped stools on shiny pedestals fronting the counter. The prep area behind included a pair of vintage Hamilton Beach milkshake machines; the sign above, in red stuck-on acrylic letters, advertised twenty flavors. The obligatory soda pop dispenser offered six choices. A standard-issue kitchen sink adorned with utensils sat beneath a Sears, Roebuck and Company clock with black filigree hands. Down the faded-yellow, much-loved Formica counter sat an old-fashioned cash register, and next to it a wire rack of chips and Fritos. Next to that, a carousel of bratwurst and hot dogs was beginning its orbit—which entrees lured us back in for lunch later that day.

What we didn't expect to find in a soda fountain was the leather tooling shop operated by the hostess's husband. Behind us in a large workroom, all manner of Western apparel hung in rows—vests and chaps, lariats, boots, work gloves, and jackets with fringe. Saddles in one or another stage of completion stood on a row of sawhorses. Pieces of tanned hide lay across an industrial sewing apparatus and cutting table. Leather scraps littered the floor. A display of Stetson hats, black and off-white (the only obvious concession to tourism we saw in Dubois) ran cheek-by-jowl in stacks of four or five across the back wall.

The few commercial businesses in town did not go the postcard-and-T-shirt route. Instead there were uncrowded curio shops, an upscale art gallery (with a gracious host, an artist himself), a modest women's wear boutique, and a newly opened coffee and latté shop run by a couple new to the trade. The coffee was OK, their business acumen and caffeine-related patois still starting up the learning curve.

Our last night in Dubois was musical and magical. We sat in the gloaming in a KOA campground, inhaling the fresh, high-mountain air perfumed by campfire smoke drifting overhead like gossamer. Gold-and-green foothills backlit by snow-covered peaks glittered under an early-evening sky. Holding forth on a stage beneath a picnic shelter was a homegrown string band. No amateurs, the fiddler and the guitarist were the vocalists. A mandolin plucker accompanied them, as did, best of all, fifteen-year-old Emily. Expressionless as a sphinx, the young lady took full measure of a stand-up bass taller than she was. All in all, a calendar poster photo of an unpretentious Rocky Mountain town.

But I'm getting ahead of myself. Before the idyllic final evening in Dubois, we experienced an entirely different "poster child" of the environs. And hardly an endangered species.

2

Behemoths

We were able to spend only one night at the Jakey's Fork bed-and-breakfast. Carolyn, our hostess, had told us at the outset that she was expecting guests from England who'd made reservations long in advance. She was able to find us other lodging, however. Just south of Dubois was the Longhorn Ranch Lodge & RV Resort—part cabins, part motel, part campground. The accommodations were pine-tree picturesque, the staff was friendly, and the Wind River circled the property on the east, a short walk away.

The air smelled mountain sweet as we coasted to a stop up a dirt drive. A momma scurried her troop of tiny ducklings out of our path. Songbirds serenaded a gentle welcome. We unpacked and ensconced ourselves in Adirondack chairs on the porch. As we closed our eyes and began to relax into the peace of the morning, the first of a brood of invasive species drove in.

A *vehiculus behemoth*, up close and in living color, came lumbering toward us. Coffee mugs suspended mid-sip, we could only stare as the beast, one of the most plentiful critters in the Rockies, rumbled slowly past. We craned our necks upward to see whether it would clear the overhead trees.

My neighbor's fifth wheel and your father's Airstream, even the large ones, are dwarfed nowadays by land cruisers the size of boxcars. Scary, and huge enough when cautiously overtaken on the highway, each one that rolled slowly past us over the course of the day blotted out the sun. And instead of a smiling driver in a familiar blue Greyhound bus, hat tipped back, there was a sausage of a guy with a full six feet of headroom over his chrome dome.

Dual rear axles are mandatory. Optional, but common enough, are pop-out rooms that become rectangular promontories extruding from the side to enlarge an already commodious living space. The interior design in some models, I'm told, qualifies for a *House Beautiful* centerfold. Gaspingly expensive, these leviathans are glossy and sleek, like a pop star's road-tour bus. The largest and glitziest, fully loaded, can be yours for half a million bucks, minimum.

They kept on coming, no two models alike. By afternoon, the place was like a dry land yacht harbor; surely there'd be a juried competition later for whose floating showroom was the longest, the cleanest, the most shipshape, with a special category for originality. By nightfall, several dozen of the breed had collected at Longhorn Ranch. They'd play well together, we hoped.

We watched as one fellow peered out the slide-back captain's window and began to maneuver his rig into its assigned anchorage, a slot as narrow as a bowling lane and overgrown by trees. He powered off and lowered himself out of the pilot seat. With whitish hair coming out from under the band at the neck of his ball cap, he was indistinguishable from his fellows (drivers under sixty-five, it seems, need not apply)—same shiny, round head and beach-ball paunch, and bib overalls (the "Wyoming tuxedo"). When he walked around to unfasten the steps and hook up the power and on-site septic, he didn't need to stoop to clear the side mirror. His head barely topped the wheel well. How on earth did his feet reach the pedals?

Muffled snickers from the curious onlookers, hands stuffed into the bibs of their overalls, possibly echoed my thoughts. They continued until the fellow's copilot dismounted. She wore olive-drab Bermuda shorts and a turquoise tube top that bulged in too many places. No taller than her companion, she walked around and, hands on her hips, faced down the skeptics. One glare must have sufficed because the group of nosy clones dispersed. Size doesn't matter, it seems, when it comes to giants of the roadway. I awarded the couple's glamorous motorhome pride of place at Longhorn Ranch Lodge.

Now there is much to be said on the positive side of the ledger about RV life—retirement on the road, visiting national park after battlefield after interesting town (e.g., Dubois), et cetera, and somehow learning to reckon with sticker shock at every stop for petrol. Writer Ann Patchett once regretted, at first, accepting an assignment to take a Wyoming and Montana road trip in a Winnebago. By the time she wrote her essay, she'd had second thoughts:

> [I'd reluctantly agreed to drive a] lumbering road buffalo on highways so narrow I wouldn't dare pass a Miata. If you're going to drive a house, why not stay home?
>
> [But by the end of our trip], I feel like I went out to report on the evils of crack and have come back with a butane torch and a pipe. I went undercover to expose a cult and have returned in saffron robes with my head shaved. I have fallen in love with my recreational vehicle …
>
> Under various awnings there are indoor-outdoor carpeting, potted plants and wind chimes, beautiful patio furniture, a large stuffed bear on a folding chair holding an American flag. In the morning the air fills with the smell of eggs and sausage. It's like a neighborhood in an imaginary version of the 1950s, with a virtuous respectability so kitschy, so obvious, one longs to mock it, except I can't anymore.

I strolled the grounds that evening, the peace and quiet lightly decibelled by idling refrigeration units. The newest fad among the land cruiser crowd at Longhorn Ranch seemed to be placing an outline of tiny lights, à la Christmas but blue or white, around on the ground to enclose one's own space, his or her perimeter inside of which were the sort of accoutrements Ann Patchett described. This was not meant to exclude, but rather enclose, like maybe one's backyard at home. Inside the colorful boundary and around the campfire, marshmallows a-roasting, a family would sit and softly sing camp songs. I couldn't argue with the ambience, but I did wonder how many still had brick-and-mortar homes with backyards along with the mobile domesticity on display. Not that it was any of my business.

That said, there was one frightening incident the next morning. A pair of late-arriving campers had pitched their pup tent after dark in a campsite too close to a land whale. Bright and early, the leviathan rumbled to life while the campers still slept. The monster began to lumber forward without noticing the insignificant obstacle in its path. Only a terrified cry from the tent kept its occupants from being crushed under the tires like a discarded McDonalds burger box. No one died.

I strolled around the camp that morning, past the busy horseshoe pit, my goal being to check on the Wind River. It was still there, I guessed about fifty feet across. The bank was thick with ankle-high grass. Fronds of dark-green ferns and scrub bushes overhung the river's emerald, near-shore edge. A pair of mergansers stayed close to the bank in the shelter of a mass of driftwood. Out farther, midriver, ribbons of sand lay here and there just under the surface despite the steady and strong current. It'd be a challenging pull upstream. After rapids plunging thousands of feet down the mountains, the Wind River was enjoying the flat valley and gentle grade.

On the way back through the grounds, I once again marveled at the sizes and varieties, the unabashed ostentation of RVdom, and unconcerned domesticity. I came upon a dog, securely tied up, thankfully, that set up a noisy racket. It was not a big dog, but an indeterminate breed with a scruffy gray-and-white coat. I was wary, but the owner shushed him and assured me I was safe.

"What's the dog's name?" I asked.

"Faulkner," he said.

"Faulkner? Now that's novel," said I, pun intended. "How'd you decide on that?"

"Cuz he's full of sound, and furry."

I yelped, myself. Never judge a person by his coveralls. Or his patented Stetson, his maroon braces, or his brown, scuffed Wellingtons.

"That line is from Macbeth" was my clever riposte. "Why didn't you name him that?"

"The wife said he'd be double the toil and trouble."

Ouch! I was in over my head. But in for a penny, etc. "You gave in."

"Yeah, I washed my hands of the whole thing."
Why did I think he'd been waiting years for some rube to wander by and lob literary softballs to him? I declined his offer of a beer and slunk back to the cabin.

The next morning, we went in search of a more traditional species, a mammalian, nonmechanized icon of the Rockies. A species for which rivers and mountains and towns are named.

3

Bighorns, the Critters

The Wind River Range is home to one of the largest herds of bighorn sheep in the country. We drove south of Dubois one morning in search of the legendary critters. Trail Lake Road, improved dirt and gravel, took us into the mountains. Around each curve was yet another expanse of Rocky Mountain scenery— hillsides and valleys with wildflowers of every color, staggering granite escarpments and forested mountainsides, and far-off, snow-capped peaks outlined against an untroubled sky. A chain of five glistening, cobalt-blue lakes led to the Whiskey Mountain Habitat Area, one of the largest bighorn sheep wintering areas. The road ended at a turnaround, a trailhead that led into the wilderness. We parked … and gaped. The stunning stillness was broken only by the trickle of a creek far below us and a nearby grove of quaking aspen fluttering in the light breeze.

I'd only seen a bighorn sheep in the wild once. Driving south out of Banff one summer after a visit to that wonderful Canadian national park, I happened upon a big old fella standing in the middle of the road. My destination that morning had been Radium Hot Springs, British Columbia. The town lies along the Columbia River, still only a modest waterway flowing north from its headwaters at Lake Windermere before reaching Kinbasket Lake where it makes a surprising U-turn back toward the south and the States. According to my handy guidebook, seven hundred and seventy-seven hardy folks called Radium Hot Springs home. It lay just ahead, I was hungry, and I needed a break from negotiating miles of serpentine highway.

My guidebook had told me that Radium Hot Springs didn't miss any chances to capitalize on the local ovine talent, Rocky Mountain Bighorn Sheep, *Ovis canadensis*. There's an annual event called the Headbanger Festival in November. The Park Service offers tourists a HEAD BANGER TOUR—$15 ADULTS, $12 CHILDREN. Chaperones, pepper spray, prepared trails, all good. Hooray for the Chamber of Commerce. But encountering a signature example of the breed in person, unsupervised as it were, would be different. What if it was mating season? Who could you ask?

Meeting up with large wildlife in any circumstances in the actual out-of-doors … well, everyone has a story: The bear and the food "safely" strung up in the tree; an angry muskrat cornered on the trail; even a gutsy doe standing her ground by her fawns. But aren't forest denizens wary of highways?

Not this specimen, who looked all of the 250 pounds they're said to reach and sometimes exceed. Vertical cliffs rose on one side of the highway, and precipitous drop-offs disappeared on the other. Concentrating on the road had been difficult enough amid the majestic scenery of the Kootenay Rockies. Then, there he was, my new best friend, blocking both lanes.

He didn't give way—just stood there staring at me, then looked over his shoulder at an oncoming vehicle that had stopped, driver's door open, with a fellow taking a photograph. The beast turned back to me and eyed my black pickup truck. He was brawny, buff-colored, and stood four feet tall at the top of his remarkable headgear that can weigh thirty pounds— enormous, curved, rough-ridged horns that say, "Yes. We mean business!" (A ewe's horns are much smaller.) Noted for keen vision, the fellow had yellow eyes with menacing black slits for pupils. I watched for the first telltale movement of a hoof. They don't call them rams for nothing.

What to do if this guy decided I was a rival or an unwelcome interloper? Surely he didn't think I was going to horn in on his harem. Even if not yet into rutting season, could he be thinking my front bumper would be something he might have a go at? Practice up, maybe. The truck's bumper being butted by horns twice the weight of a bowling ball—moving at over twenty miles per hour—would put a dent in my deductible at the very least.

We compromised. I didn't wave a bright-colored cape to shoo him away. I did put the truck in reverse, just in case. I leaned out the window and said, "Have a nice day, kind sir." Bored no doubt, my adversary walked coolly to the edge of the road, where he stopped, squatted, and irrigated a surprisingly large plot of Kootenay Forest real estate. Dismissively, I thought. Then, with the scuff of a hoof, he jumped onto an invisible track up the cliff and disappeared. I was not worth his trouble, thankfully.

However, here's where this anecdote gets unfunny. Ancestors of bighorn sheep crossed the Bering Land Bridge from Siberia seven hundred fifty thousand years ago. Since that time, disease passed along by cattle and mindless hunting—often to deprive Native Americans of a food product, as also happened with buffalo—drove the species nearly to extinction. In Lakota Sioux, *hechinskayapi,* (pronounced "hay-cheen-shkah-yah-pee") means "spoon horns" and refers to the outsized crowns from which spoons and scoops were carved. (The Absaroka Sioux name is *ahsahta,* meaning "big head.")

Today, there are fewer than seventy thousand sheep, down from one and a half or two million at the beginning of the nineteenth century. Canadian bighorns are not as much at risk since populations of *canadensis* have been restored and are clustered in a narrow band extending from northern British Columbia southward through parts of the Rockies. But Sierra Nevada sheep are listed as endangered. A Badlands subspecies of bighorn, native to the Dakotas, has been extinct since 1926.

Scientists guesstimate that, as a general rule, a given species of mammal will stick around for a million years or so on average. How are *homo sapiens* doing? Intelligent ancestors of ours showed up about two hundred thousand years ago; those with rudimentary communicative speech, fifty thousand years. Our earliest written tablets appeared a little over five thousand years ago. The Declaration of Independence was written about five minutes ago. On this scale, the near extinction of bighorn sheep took around two minutes, thanks to us.

I restarted the truck and drove on, slowly, in tribute to a majestic mountain sheep, the original headbanger, who'd treated me with the disdain my species deserved.

This day, near Dubois in the Whiskey Mountain Habitat Area, we were unlucky. No sheep. We scanned the hillsides and cliffs with binoculars. A faraway dot would turn out to be a tree or a boulder. The green, grassy expanses were empty. We were too late, we were told. Lambing had ended in May, and ewes and their offspring had moved to higher elevations. God keep them safe.

4

Confluencing

Confluence, (verb transitive or intransitive): To be intensely fascinated, perhaps obsessively, by the phenomenon—hydraulic, historic, and harmonious—of the merging of two rivers. E.g., "Today, we plan to confluence Jakey's Fork and the Wind River."

To follow the succession of rivers beginning with Jakey's Fork, we trusted that we would find mileposts or indications of some sort along the way where each tributary joined a larger river. There'd be a place, a promontory or a bluff or a sandy bank, where we'd get out of the car, stretch, and gaze at the natural event: the confluence of two important waterways. We'd feel in our bones the significance, natural and memorable, of those landmarks. Each such joining of waters would surely be recognized in some way, perhaps with formal signage, maybe even a little park. How could it not be! We found out.

Companionable Jakey's Fork had tantalized us as it raced along just beyond the deck of Butch Cassidy's bunkhouse where we'd spent the night. The sound had lulled us to sleep. After cascading from the heights at Union Pass, Jakey's would join the Wind River not far from the driveway to Carolyn's bed-and-breakfast.

We pulled off and parked by a bridge that spanned the creek near its junction with the river. We heard the rush of the water beyond the trees. The Wind had to be no more than fifty yards away. I set off to do a little bushwhacking. Cherie waited by the car, 9-1-1 on speed dial just in case—a needless precaution, of course. I started down an overgrown fishermen's path, pushing aside tree limbs and wading through waist-high grass, then more branches and deer brush and thorn bushes. As I plowed ahead, following the sound, I smelled the musky dampness of bigger water.

After twenty minutes of sweeping branches away from my eyes, stumbling across rocks, tripping over roots, and twice nearly face-planting down muddy slopes, I gave up. The overgrown shrubbery, chest-high dead-ends, and fallen logs were relentless. Abandoned barbed wire is not the best handhold if one loses his balance. The noisy river, out there just beyond the next bunch of tangled thickets, just laughed.

I retreated and took my scraped and scratched body back to the car. So much for a landmark. No sign, no notice, no luck … no nothing. I felt like I'd attended the rehearsal dinner but missed the wedding.

Back at the car, Cherie Polysporined and bandaged a small gash on my forehead, a larger one on my elbow. She tended to my ego. There would be other opportunities, she pointed out. My fruitless hacking through underbrush, she assured me, would be the exception, not the rule. With good maps, open country ahead, and the classic *Smithsonian Guide to Natural America* on the console between us, we'd carry on.

As we drove away, however, a fantasy, perhaps a bit of revenge, occurred to me. What if I were to drop a Ping-Pong ball into Jakey's Fork next to our cabin? I'd inscribe it in indelible ink in very tiny script, "NOLA or bust!" and add my email address, then give it a toss. From there we could follow the little sphere's inevitable path all the way to New Orleans and the Gulf of Mexico. After four thousand miles of floating and bobbing and racing and ducking under branches and past curious fishermen—the Ping-Pong ball, not us—we'd catch up to it from time to time, or vice versa, and wave it on its epic way.

Environmental correctness prevailed. Plus, Cherie flashed me that familiar look, one eyebrow raised, whereby not so much my judgment but my sanity was being questioned. However, she persuaded me, pointing out the unlikelihood that our emissary could negotiate logjams, dikes and dams, rapids, slow drifts through lakes, and meddling children if it floated too close to shore. Lake Sakakawea in North Dakota, for example, is almost two hundred miles long all by itself. The trip would take years. Her rock-solid logic carried the day.

Bloodied and not a little unbowed, we went into Dubois for another yummy lunch. That night at Longhorn Ranch, I counted Ping-Pong balls instead of sheep and fell asleep safely ensconced among snoozing behemoths. We set off the next morning tracking the Wind River, with gentle Dubois, Wyoming, in the rearview mirror, sandwiches, Fritos, and an Oreo snack-pack in the hamper, and Diet Cokes in the ice chest. "SE" said the dashboard readout.

At this point, it's worth explaining what it was about the actual confluence of rivers that had me hooked. The word is used here frequently because good synonyms are scarce: junction, convergence, joining, intersection, linkage, union? Confluence is a fine word, certainly, and suits the purpose of writing about rivers, but there's a childhood-of-origin etymology all its own.

Students who didn't doze off in American History will recall that, upstream from Sacramento, California, on the American River, there sat a sawmill owned by a Swiss fellow named Johan Sutter. In January of 1848, a hired hand from New Jersey named James Marshall noticed shiny orange flecks of metal in the millrace. He knew it was gold. "Eureka!" he reportedly shouted, quoting Archimedes. "Look what I found!" And California was discovered in earnest.

To be sure, for centuries European seafaring explorers—Vancouver, Cabrillo—knew of California. They'd sailed along the California coast and, giving the Farallon Islands wide berth, had missed the Golden Gate. In the eighteenth century the intrepid Father Junipero Serra, traveling north from Mexico, established Catholic missions a day's journey apart, from San Diego to San Francisco. Even the Russians, in 1812, had crossed the Bering Strait and built Fort Ross in today's Sonoma County. But it was James Marshall's discovery that ignited the Gold Rush and began to invent the State of California.

Johan Sutter had built a fort in Sacramento in 1839—a centerpiece of the colony he founded and named New Helvetia—not far from where the American River joins the Sacramento River. My mother and I used to refer to the landmark as being near the "conflagration" of the two rivers ... which drove my lawyer father to distraction.

Conflagration just sounded so much better than confluence, notwithstanding that few things have as little to do with a conflagration as a waterway—excepting the Cuyahoga River, of course. For a while my dad would correct us, then he'd just shake his head and give up. Mom and I used the word often in ridiculous contexts, and it remained our little joke. ("Hey, watch out at the conflagration of those two grocery aisles up ahead.")

The preceding utterly gratuitous digression is not profound, but the correct word eventually stuck. Thus, to mark our passage and a river's route from one place to another, finding confluences made sense, touchstones for our exploration.

The magic of rivers begins, in my mind, with the disconnect between the modest beginnings of creeks and streams and the mighty masses of water they become. Tens of thousands of capillaries and veins nourish this water planet we inhabit and make their way to the oceans, which hold 96 percent of the earth's water. Try to picture tectonic plates floating around the globe on oceans of water. To be sure, they float on magma as well, but less than a third of the time.

All rivers begin inauspiciously. In the Rockies, as elsewhere, crystal droplets slip out from under a melting snowpack. Several more trickle out of other clumps of snow and collect in a rivulet no wider than the width of a shoe. Together with others they become the silver beginnings of a creek. Sometimes, in a high meadow like Union Pass, springs are fed by an aquifer higher up that seeps underground before silently filling a crystal-clear pond. The pond overflows at its lowest extremity and water, doing what water does, heads downhill.

From there, something we'd call a creek tumbles and burbles over icy rocks until it enters a flat, high-mountain marsh where acres of impenetrable vegetation—snowberry, elderberry, rushes, buffalo berry, sedges, and smartweed—hide the secret water beneath. Insects, songbirds, newts and frogs, beaver, otter, and deer keep vigil, as the stream is incubated in this hidden womb. Gaining strength and reemerging, the water negotiates switchbacks and oxbows, often doubling back on itself as it meanders. Whereupon, something called a river leaves its marshy upland and begins its rush down the mountain. It swirls around boulders, is dammed by logs and leaves, and collects in pools where fingerlings grow.

From whiskery sourdoughs panning for gold in the Mother Lode to the brook filling the pond at Grandma's farm, to the whisk of a fly fisherman where a river runs through, or to my dad and I dangling salmon eggs in front of hopefully hungry trout, the charm of a stream is bewitching. There are no colors more brilliant than yellow and orange and brick-red pebbles and wisps of algae refracted by sunlight through the glaze of a still, transparent pool.

Miles later, tired and slow as it cruises the flatland seeking the sea, a river's legacy is timelessness—a timelessness that can be felt by simply dipping a hand in and holding it against the current. The eighteenth-century hymnist Isaac Watts compared Time itself to "an ever-flowing stream." "A thousand ages in thy sight/Are like an evening gone," he wrote.

More than once, whether crossing bridges or small culverts, Cherie and I would think of the quiet, private beginnings at Union Pass and compare it to a full-blown river large enough to carry canoes, even steamboats. The particular ever-flowing stream we started with would eventually become the mighty Mississippi, the breadth and strength of which aquatic leviathan is astonishing to anyone who crosses it, particularly by boat.

"The man of wisdom delights in water" (Confucius). As a person who needs all the wisdom he can scrounge up, I shook off the defeat at the confluence of Jakey's Fork and the Wind River. We moved on down the road to the appropriately named Riverton, Wyoming.

The name promised not one nor two, but three junctions: The "big" Wind River, which we'd been following, the Little Wind River entering from the west, and the *Popo Agee*. A Crow Indian word meaning "burbling waters," the *Popo Agee* rises in the Shoshone National Forest. The river famously disappears into a cavern of limestone rock underground, then reappears downstream a mere quarter-mile away after two hours! (Did they use a stopwatch and Ping-Pong ball to figure that out?)

Feeling that the odds were in our favor, we drove into town and began to look around.

5

What's in a Name

We drove through Riverton, Wyoming, eyes peeled for helpful signs. Surely, at least where the Wind River and the Popo Agee met would be well marked. We consulted our map. We went through town, then into the outskirts. On a hunch and by dead reckoning we located a rutted gravel road that looked promising. It led us to a dammed up and uninviting swimming hole, but no river. The road did disappear into a copse of trees in a likely direction, but heavy chain barred the way, as did a sign next to it: No Unauthorized Vehicles.

If missing the confluence of Jakey's Fork and the Wind River was strike one, this was strike two.

We didn't even turn off the car. Back through Riverton we drove in a huff. With Cherie at the wheel, I made mental notes of the uninviting roadside attractions we passed—a half-empty strip mall, a boarded-up A & W, an auto-wrecking yard, a forlorn realty office with an Open sign in the window, tattered, white plastic bags flapping in the trees. We even passed a septic truck with the words stenciled on the tank, #1 IN #2—Have Hose Will Travel. You can't make up stuff like that. If, as the man said, reality is the stage manager of life, Riverton deserves a Tony.

The newly enlarged Wind River made a sharp pivot at Riverton and turned north. The highway followed the river. Immediately beyond the dam at Boysen Reservoir was the Wind River Canyon. Our spirits improved. It was the river itself that was restorative. Of course.

A marvel of geology cutting through the Owl Creek

43

Mountains, the thirty-four-mile-long canyon was created by tectonic plate shifts; the Wind River itself was just along for the ride. Beneath roadside cliffs rising to twenty-five hundred feet, our narrow roadway snaked along, squeezed in by the river, yet somehow leaving room for active railroad tracks. A driver or two with a death wish tried to pass us. The sun, high in the sky, dodged in and out from behind escarpments and glinted off the dashboard. Occasionally, a turnout would allow for fishing access, but parking was precarious so we didn't stop. We actually relaxed on a lovely drive past frothy rapids and glass-topped pools of dark jade.

When we exited the north end of Wind River Canyon, lo and behold, we were on a different river! Correction: same river, new name. No longer the Wind River, it had become the Bighorn.

No confluence had taken place, just a geographic mistake corrected by the stroke of a cartographer's pen. The spot now charmingly called "The Wedding of the Waters" is not so much a place as a thought. Two rivers' names were not sleight-of-hand, rather the result of a miscommunication among nineteenth-century explorers with a lot else on their minds. The river that disappeared into the Wind River chasm twenty-five sinuous miles to the south wasn't known for several years to be the same one that flowed out into open prairie to the north. According to writer John McPhee, even natives didn't put one and one together. By the time the error was discovered, both rivers had names, and they stuck until later exploration of the canyon set everyone straight.

Names. As a communicative species, what we call things speaks volumes. From Rumpelstiltskin to rhinoceros, images flash into our minds. But what to make of *chwewamink*, a Delaware Indian word meaning "large prairie place" or "at the big river flat." Say it quickly enough, as white newcomers did, and it comes out "Wyoming." But mispronunciation isn't the end of this etymological story. The name eased its way into popular culture via an odd confluence of its own. Fact or fiction? Turns out, both.

Delaware Indians in the Far West? As any Keystone Stater can attest, *Chwewamink*, the original "Wyoming Valley," lies along the Susquehanna River in northeastern Pennsylvania near Wilkes-Barre. Nonetheless, a US congressman, Representative James Ashley of Ohio, a native of Pennsylvania, in 1865 proposed to Congress the anglicized Native American name for the newly created, far-off Wyoming Territory.

Ashley was fond of a popular poem "Gertrude of Wyoming," written by a Scotsman, Thomas Campbell, in 1809. A contemporary of Walter Scott, Wordsworth, Coleridge, and Washington Irving, Campbell had only a vague notion of Pennsylvania—or anywhere else in the young United States, for that matter. He placed the poetic Wyoming on the Atlantic coast, choosing as his subject the killing of over three hundred "provincials," i.e., Americans, on July 3, 1778. On that tragic date during the Revolutionary War, British and Iroquois forces led by one Joseph Brant—originally a Mohawk named *Thayendanagea* —descended on a peaceful settlement and slaughtered the innocent inhabitants.

Poetic license is one thing, but one can wonder why Campbell chose the tragedy as his subject—typical anti-English Scot that he was, perhaps? What we do know is that he describes Wyoming as a

> Sweet land! may I thy lost delights recall,
> And paint thy Gertrude in her bowers of yore,
> Whose beauty was the love of Pennsylvania's
> shore!

Gertrude? Who in the world was *Gertrude*?

For thirty-nine florid stanzas, the poet tells us who. It seems that a fellow named Albert was the "judge and patriarch" of the pioneer settlement where the massacre took place. Gertrude was his adored, one and only child. In popular Romantic fashion, an orphaned boy is taken in by Albert and then disappears from the narrative to travel abroad. Lengthy, bucolic descriptions of Wyoming and the fair Gertrude continue. Then the young lad returns and, no surprise, is bewitched by the lass and weds her. After only three months of connubial bliss— barely disguised in good Jane Austen style—the "Monster Brant," as he's later known, shows up and commits his atrocities.

The poem was well received in the newly independent United States, and the name Wyoming took its place in the young nation's lore. While Congressman Ashley can be forgiven for being a fan of poet Campbell, his rudimentary knowledge of geography led him, along with Campbell, astray. He had second thoughts after actually visiting the new territory far to the west, where he found the environs to be quite unlike what he'd expected. No surprise. He tried to retract the name, but too late. In 1868, Wyoming was officially designated a US territory; statehood followed in 1890.

One assumes Gertrude was pleased.

One last digression on names. As students of Native American culture can well remind us, starry denizens high in the heavens have Arab, Roman, or Greek names: Aldebaran and Altair, Ares and Orion, Sirius and Cassiopeia, Rigel, Betelgeuse, the planets Mars and Venus, and on and on. But here on terra firma, the ground under our feet is called Nebraska, Iowa, Illinois, Alaska. No fewer than twenty-six states have names derived from one Indian language or another, not to mention countless towns, rivers, deserts, mountains, and valleys.

The strangest etymology of all, perhaps, is that for the state of Oregon. Experts disagree about how the word came to be. Did British explorer Johanthan Carver, in 1778, during one of many expeditions searching for the "Great River of the

West," misunderstand the Shoshone words *Ogwa Pe-On* where the "gwa" is pronounced like an "r"? Or, was "Ouaricon" or "Ouragon" a typographer's error on a speculative 1715 map and mistaken for the Ohio or some other river in the upper Midwest? Turning to European provenance, how about *ouragan*, the French word for hurricane? Possibly, bastardized "oregano" or "Aragon," or the Spanish name for a "big ornamented-ear," the name given to an indigenous population called "Orejon"? Take your pick.

For what it's worth, by 1804 Thomas Jefferson's instructions to Lewis and Clark included exploration of the "Columbia, Oregon, Colorado, or any other river." By then, the names "Oregon Territory" and "Oregon" were familiar. Just as certainly, no such "Ouaricon" River, however spelled or pronounced, ever existed. Bernard DeVoto called it "a product of pure thought." If anything, the river Jefferson had in mind turned out to be not the "Oregon" and was named the Columbia.

Thus, and turning the immortal Heraclitus on his head, the Wind/Bighorn was the same river after all; the same river with two names, in a state with an invented name that at least hadn't been called "Gertrude."

6

Wyoming

Wyoming is a beautiful state, one of our favorites, and a place of contrasts—topographical, political, and sartorial.

Less than a week before, in well under an hour we'd dropped out of the thin air at 9,660 foot Togowotee Pass down to Dubois, nestled at three thousand four hundred feet. The highway leaving the Wind River Canyon, at four thousand feet, took us through the wide-open expanse of the Bighorn Basin. Before the day was out, we would climb above nine thousand feet in the Bighorn Mountains.

We stopped for lunch in a city park in the town of Thermopolis and picnicked beside the river. The temperature hovered in the nineties, but a shaded table under quaking aspen and next to the shushing of the river refreshed us after half a day's drive from Dubois and through Riverton. The Wyoming Dinosaur Center is in Thermopolis—a harbinger of things to come, it turned out. We munched our sandwiches and slurped our soda pops not far from a tall, quite fetching stegosaurus. We dawdled awhile, then waved to a patient park employee astride his idling mower and packed up.

In 1869, Wyoming became the first state in the country to grant women the right to vote, well before the Nineteenth Amendment to the US Constitution was ratified in 1920. Wyoming can also boast the first female governor in the nation, Nellie Tayloe Ross, who took the oath of office in 1925. In more conservative 2016, billboards of red, white, and blue featured the smiling face of Republican Liz Cheney, running for Wyoming's one and only seat in the US House of Representatives.

The Cowboy State has yet to adopt anti-smoking-in-or-near-restaurants laws. When taking a stroll after dinner, the perfume of burning tobacco tainted the breeze … to the detriment of an otherwise pleasant meal.

Wyoming is a state of cowboy hats, boots, and chaps. Also black leather biker vests, with motorcycles to match. Or camo jeans and shirts on men and women and kids. Cherie's travel costume—black slacks, orange short-sleeved cotton blouse, and knockabouts—didn't stand out too much. By contrast, yours truly, adventurous Western Washingtonian that I am, made a fashion statement in khaki shorts, a T-shirt with the name of the place where we stayed the night before, my Friday Harbor baseball hat, and Teva sandals. No one commented, that I could tell.

Contrasts were everywhere. Even rivers in Wyoming, according to John McPhee, "pretend" to flow in one direction, then change their mind. "In fact," he claims, "there is no obvious relationship between most of the major rivers in Wyoming and the landscapes they traverse … [They] seem to argue with nature as well as with common sense …"

We set our course by the newly christened Bighorn which seemed to be behaving itself, meandering through flat countryside. Flat prairies, scattered with sagebrush and Russian olive trees, were punctuated by calendar-photo barns and fences. Green pastures lapped up against rocky cliffs. Rolling hills lay in the foreground, dusky-blue mountains beyond them. Distant, sky-high mountain ranges were topped with snow. Every so often we'd pass a sheer escarpment of "badland," striated bluffs, a kaleidoscope of crimson and orange and yellow—sedimentary sand, silt, and clay compressed over millions of years, now exposed by wind and water.

Ahead was the Bighorn Canyon National Recreation Area which straddles the Wyoming-Montana border. A reservoir snakes through the canyon for seventy-two miles, backed up behind Yellowtail Dam, attracting boaters of all stripes and tempting hikers along easy or precipitous trails. The park even sponsors an artist-in-residence program. We would explore it the following day after spending the night in an inauspicious small town called Lovell. Or so we thought.

If "inauspicious" means empty streets, few cars, and fewer people, then Lovell is its poster child. But small and sleepy even by rural Wyoming standards, the hoped-for night's rest was soon the furthest thing from our minds. Road-weary and hungry after a long drive, we patrolled the town looking for our motel, the not surprisingly named "Cattleman." One pass down Main Street was followed by another, necks craning, searching in all directions. No Cattleman. No other motel in town, period. We circled a block for a second time and pulled over to double-check the name. I rifled through a file in the backseat and found the address. We had to be in the right place. We looked again and both saw it at the same time. We looked at each other, openmouthed. Could that be the Cattleman? Right across the street?

Though featured on a certain internet search engine I'd used, this "motel" was freaky. Not quite Norman Bates-y, what we stared at was a dreary, one-story house in a low-rent neighborhood. Next to a scrabbly lawn the size of a postage-stamp was a driveway lined with chipped, gray cinder blocks, the kind used in freeway construction. There was no indication the place was even a motel until we saw atop a tall white pole, paint peeling and rusty, the barely readable words "Vacancy/ No Vacancy," letters askew. We saw no lobby, no drive-thru, no sign of life. The windows were dark. In short, it looked like a once-upon-a-time rest home that'd been shuttered. There was, in fact, what looked like a broken gurney parked behind the building.

I punched in the phone number. A sleepy woman answered. She confirmed that we had indeed found the right place. I mumbled an excuse about "plans changing, etc." and cancelled the reservation. We'd be charged for the room anyway, she said. No surprise, since we figured we were the only guests the place was likely to see for a while.

Now what to do?

It was early evening. The sun was still high in the western sky and, air-conditioning or not, the day hadn't cooled off. The nearest town was miles away, and behind us. I muttered, and thought about choice words for the review I would post on the Motels-Are-Us website. Cherie, ever practical, suggested we at least move along and not stay parked across the street from Lovell's wannabe hospitality center. We pulled away.

At which point, Fortune smiled upon us in the form of modern technology and a savvy young fellow at a service station we pulled into back on Main Street. In his early twenties with casually mussed sandy hair and alert blue eyes (the gal inside at the cash register surely dreamed of him on her walk home), he wore oil-stained coveralls with a gasoline logo. After wiping his hands on a paper towel, our New Best Friend proceeded to save our bacon.

After listening to our tale of woe and instantly agreeing with our assessment of the local lodging situation, he went to work on his smart phone. In less than five minutes, he not only scoped out an accommodation at a lodge up the road in the Bighorn Mountains but also got my OK, then went ahead and confirmed our reservations—using his credit card.

There are angels!

7

Bighorns, the Mountains

After the letdown in Lovell, we still had miles to go before we slept, and, it turned out, a memorable climb. Across Bighorn Lake and the flat, oval-shaped basin carved by the river, a skyscraping massif loomed ahead of us, growing nearer by the mile. The Bighorn range of mountains, somewhat of an outlier, hangs like an appendage off the eastern edge of the main breadth of the Rockies—a sudden, nine-thousand-foot-tall appendage.

An increasing number of road signs alerted us to the upcoming grade. The climb began on gentle switchbacks, then became more pronounced. Up and up we drove around S-curves and loops, mile after higher mile. We'd occasionally get a glimpse out the window of a roadway high above us, shored up by a concrete retaining wall, carved into the hillside like it was on stilts. Then it would disappear from view, blocked by an intervening rock cliff. Adventurous mountaineers, their colorful ropes a-dangling while rappelling down a forbidding façade, wouldn't have been a surprise. Eye-catching vistas far below tempted us to take our eyes off the road.

We passed no trailers or RVs, only a pair of hardy construction trucks. The vertical elevation gain over the next eighteen and a half miles was over five thousand feet—and over a linear distance of five miles west to east as the crow flew. The climb was educational as well as entertaining. Along with truck runaway ramps ("arrester beds" in the lingo), "steep grade -10%," and "sharp curve" signs, roadside markers announced the ever-younger geologic ages we passed through: Cambrian, Ordovician, Mississippian, Pennsylvanian, Permian, Jurassic, and Cretaceous. Passing craggy rock outcroppings and chiseled facings was like flipping through an earth science textbook—solid layers of granite, sandstone slumps, black basalt, and more.

An enormous swath of the northern tier of the western United States and part of Canada is a wonderland of paleontology. Five hundred and fifty million years ago, during the Cambrian Explosion, versions of most of the animal groups familiar today first showed up in the fossil record. The world's protocontinents were wandering the globe, and inland seas and marshes covered most of middle North America, creating the Carboniferous Period. Today, fossil-hunting scientists and college crews with dusty backpacks and armed with rock picks, chipping hammers, hand lenses and microscopes, tweezers and trowels, annually descend on the Badlands in South Dakota, on the Burgess Shale in British Columbia, into Dinosaur National Monument in Colorado, up onto the Uinta Plateau, and down the Green River in Utah.

Our ascent into the Bighorn Mountains ended at 9,430 feet. Higher still, at ten thousand feet, was Medicine Wheel Passage, a prehistoric Native American spiritual site. Astronomers have attached Stonehenge-like significance to the cairns at Medicine Wheel—now a National Historic Landmark—that are arranged around a central axis. It is speculated that the stones once pointed to the rising or setting of seasonal bright stars such as Sirius, Aldebaran, and Rigel, but positioned, due to the precession of the earth, as they would have been a millennium ago.

At last we reached the Bighorn Mountain Plateau. My hands relaxed on the steering wheel. We settled back and cruised along through an open alpine expanse of many lakes, trailheads, and dwindling snowpacks. The air rushing past our open windows was crisp and clean and smelled of pine and spruce. We arrived at Bear Lodge Resort, the destination where our savior back in Lovell had made reservations. Located at

Burgess Junction, the "resort" turned out to be a snowmobiler, ORV, RV, camper, and biker gathering spot smack in the middle of the forest. Hardy drivers, they.

Founded in 1929, the vintage, three-story lodge was surrounded by rustic cabins and camping sites and slots and hook-ups. A gasoline island in front with pumps that dated back to the last century was doing an understandably brisk business. (I thought I saw a faded Flying A logo.) The lodge itself was comfortable enough but showed its age—sort of like a favorite sweater with a hole in the elbow and stretched out here and there, but you still wear it.

Our welcome was gracious enough—surprising, in fact. The tall, one-armed, paper-hanging receptionist-slash-cashier suddenly stopped amid a frenzied flurry of phone messages and answering questions from passersby and staff. In midstroke, he asked us where we were from. I started to tell him and got as far as "Bellingham, Wash—"

"A Bellinghamster! No kidding," he yelled.

"Huh."

"The name's Roche." Hand extended. "Joe Roche. Ever heard of a little spot out in the San Juans?"

Yes, indeed. Joe's great-great-great grandfather, Richard Roche, served on a British survey vessel in the North Pacific in the 1850s. Somehow he got a harbor named after him on San Juan Island in the idyllic archipelago in the sound west of our home. Our Mr. Roche's details were fuzzy and quickly lapsed into a lament about what had happened to the place since it was taken over by corporate interests and a band of "thieving lawyers in Seattle" who developed it beyond all recognition. I didn't need Cherie's nudge to keep my erstwhile profession unsaid.

New friend Joe happily checked us in. We hustled our suitcases upstairs. There were patriotic candies on the pillow, wrapped in shiny cellophane American flags. More Wyoming. Downstairs, we lost no time finding the dining room. Nearly empty, it was attended by a lone waiter, a heavyset lad who sweated profusely and ran everywhere, bumping into tables and the occasional patron, then apologizing. Hungry though we were, dinner was mediocre. Selections were few, and only scraps remained in the bins at the salad bar. Ever-present eau de Wyoming cigarette smoke wafted in from the crowded bar down the hall. As other diners drifted in, more than one couple took a look around, then left. We skipped dessert, took a pass on the clink-and-jingle game room, clouded bar, noisy dart games, and communal hot tub on the deck, and went up to bed.

Bear Lodge Resort, a port of rescue to be sure, seemed to be barely getting by on a tired reputation: Familiar custom, minimal essentials, a captive audience of bikers and smokers, off-road utility vehicle enthusiasts, hikers and campers … and admittedly, desperate lodgers. Who were we to complain? Besides, the room was clean and the bed comfy.

The next morning we checked out, skipped breakfast, and set off through the forest, then down off the high plateau. Visibility was lousy. We were literally in the clouds and stayed there for miles. Through dense fog, the long, precipitous downgrade to the flatlands was even scarier than driving up had been. Same sharp curves, same rocky cliffs on one side and unseen roadside crevasses imagined on the other, we descended the same five thousand feet as on the way up. We crept down, both of us leaning over the dashboard, squinting ahead through windshield wipers fighting the wet, gray gloom. Blessedly overtaken by no one, we encountered only a few misty pairs of headlights making their cautious way up the grade toward us.

At last, the fog cleared and we pulled over, relieved, in the town of Dayton. We had a scrumptious breakfast in a plain and ordinary restaurant, a type that's become an icon of the road trips we take off the beaten track. Obligatory pickup trucks were parked out in front, a family of eight filled a long table, and an attentive waitress cheerily patrolled with coffee pot at the ready.

Restaurants such as this one in Dayton, Wyoming, seem
to make an almost studied attempt at non–"interior design." In
Blue Highways, William Least Heat-Moon ranked eateries on
system based on the number of calendars on the wall—insurance
salesman, AAA, the gas station down the street, the Grange, the
local feed store, bank giveaways, *Field & Stream*, Paco's Tacos, you
name it. A one-calendar place, he said, means don't bother. Five,
go out of your way just to eat there. He probably would have
rated the one that morning a "three-calendar restaurant." We
gave it a four. But then, we were hungry.

8

Two Hot Days in June

After our unscheduled overnight stop in the Bighorn Mountains and yummy breakfast in Dayton, Wyoming, the highway north into Montana would reconnect us with the Bighorn River which had disappeared into the National Recreation Area the day before. No improved road led through the canyon, hence the necessary detour into the mountains.

The Bighorn River itself emerged at Fort Smith, Montana, built in 1866 to protect westbound travelers along the Bozeman Trail. From there, the river wandered through southern Montana until connecting with the Yellowstone. We had high hopes. Surely there we would find an on-site confluence of those two rivers. We would stand and actually see the objective that so far had eluded us. On the way, we could take in the Little Bighorn Battlefield National Monument.

Truth be told, we almost skipped the battlefield. Would the celebrated monument be overdone? Touristy? Perhaps a maudlin encomium to poor old George Armstrong Custer, with an obligatory nod to proud Sitting Bull? Dumbed-down history?

Hot weather continued to dog us. The parking lot was full of cars and campers baking in the sun, with license plates from everywhere even though summer was officially several weeks away. Groups of people made their way along a concrete path and up a small rise to a state-of-the-art visitor center. Inside, the obligatory souvenir shop was chockablock with books, maps, jigsaw puzzles, videos, knickknacks, and brochures. There was a small movie theater, sounds of a video flickering our direction. But first impressions can be deceiving. We needn't have worried.

Tastefully done and informative, the battlefield tribute to fallen soldiers of the famous Indian war moved us. Volunteers were helpful but not intrusive. Tribe members from the nearby Crow Indian Agency gave tours. The memorial, originally called the Custer Battlefield, was renamed the Little Bighorn Battlefield National Monument in 1991 per a federal law signed by George H. W. Bush.

Outside the visitor center, we followed a winding path in the midmorning sun under cloudless skies. People moved slowly, stopping to read the plaques along the way. Their children were well behaved. Somber and simple marble headstones were set where it had been determined that a certain soldier or Indian had fallen. A tall granite obelisk, perched on a high point of land where the infamous Last Stand took place, was inscribed with the names of the American soldiers who died that day. Beneath the pillar, the remains of infantrymen who could later be identified are buried—up to half of them recent immigrants who'd enlisted to get a job.

We took our time wandering from one marker to another, helpful signs among yellow and purple wildflowers guiding us. Hot as it was, we contrasted our loose, comfortable summer attire with that of nineteenth-century soldiers on another, long-ago June day who had worn heavy uniforms and uncomfortable boots, and had carried full packs, rifles, and ammunition.

The highlight for us lay a short distance from the visitor center proper, the Indian Memorial. Dedicated in 2003, after six years of sometimes contentious cooperation between the US Park Service and regional Native American tribes, there is now a sanctuary, open to the sky. We entered in silence—in from the east, departing to the west—in the Indian custom of arriving and leaving a sacred space.

A circle of flagstone walls surrounded a spacious courtyard perhaps fifty feet across, like an amphitheater without seats. On top of one arc of the flagstone wall was a large sculpture, a silhouette in wrought iron of three Spirit Warriors in full regalia on horseback, racing as if into battle. The leader carried a bow and arrow, and his feathered war bonnet trailed behind him. A second warrior followed the first, still clambering aboard his speeding stallion. The third rider bent down over his shield to clasp the hand of a woman he was leaving behind. The trio sped along, framed in stark relief against the expansive panorama of the grassy hills and distant mountains of Montana.

On the other side of the circle, opposite the three charging warriors, was a unique and heart-wrenching feature. A rectangle, cut out of the wall and about waist-high above the dirt floor, formed a portal about two arm's lengths wide. Facing the hill and tall obelisk beyond, through this solemn opening, no one may pass except the eternal spirits of battle casualties—all causalities, all wars. A weeping wound summons the souls of all combatants in death, in an amphitheater of silence stunning in its simplicity.

Shopworn history can always use a little polishing with actual facts. So it was with the often-mythologized episode at Little Bighorn. To learn more, Cherie and I found a weathered wooden table in a shady spot away from the crowds and sat down with a book we'd bought. Two unconcerned deer tiptoed away into the cottonwoods. The only sound was a soft breeze rustling through the leaves above us. We sipped a soda and read.

The headline:

Two hundred and sixty-three soldiers in Custer's Seventh Cavalry fought on June 25, 1876, in a battle that lasted a futile thirty minutes, and all were wiped out. It is not known how many Indians they faced; estimates run to the thousands.

The backstory:

We learned that Sitting Bull, spiritual leader of his Hunkpapa band of Lakota Sioux, hadn't been part of the charge up the hill. As an elder, he had moved his family to safety. It was he, however, who'd succeeded in cobbling together an alliance of several tribes—"uncooperative" and nonreservation Indians such as Blackfoot, Cheyenne, Arapaho, Oglala, and Lakota Sioux—to draw the line against endless treaty violations, ever-encroaching white settlers, and ever-shrinking land on which they'd lived for generations.

In 1876, matters had reached an impasse. Sitting Bull and his allies watched as Bluecoats kept coming, stronger and more numerous than ever: Troops, weapons, horses, wagons, and with them, countless settlers and their families, gold-seekers, hunters. Protected by the US Army, the newcomers invaded Indian homeland and ignored treaties right and left—treaties that promised to last "as long as the river flows and the eagle flies." The first Oregon Trail wagon train had crossed the Rockies in 1842. Manifest Destiny was well underway by 1850. After the Homestead Act of 1862, straight lines and grids and mining claims began to define territory, not watercourses, hills, or mountains.

In 1869, at Promontory Point in Utah, locomotives of the Union Pacific and Central Pacific railroads faced one another and officials pounded into the ground a golden spike to celebrate the first transcontinental railroad. In the early 1870s, incursions by the Northern Pacific Railroad into Sioux territory met strong and bloody resistance. Then gold was discovered in the Black Hills in the Dakota Territory—sacred Sioux land—and the onslaught picked up speed.

Indian tribes had fought one another for generations before the white man came, but this was a threat they couldn't imagine—construction of forts, trained armed forces, an unlimited supply of firearms. Sporadic warfare with the US Army had gone on for years, with massacres of innocents on both sides, and more and more bloody incidents kept occurring. The deciding confrontation on a hillside overlooking the Little Bighorn River in June of 1876, or one like it, was inevitable. It was time to stand and fight.

Custer's troops were massacred, of course, but the battle,

regardless of the victor, turned out to be the beginning of the end—in hindsight, the inevitable defeat of Native Americans on the Plains and in the Rockies.

They won the fight but would, classically, lose the war. Following Custer's defeat, Sitting Bull and his allies were undone by the extent of national outrage at the annihilation of a Civil War hero and more than two hundred of his compatriots. But what a contrast in protagonists … as we would learn.

9

Hunkpapa Sioux

George Armstrong Custer, last in his class at West Point and twice court-martialed, had an eye for publicity and the media for most of his career. Not quite six feet tall and sporting distinctive, long golden locks he perfumed with cinnamon oil, he wore his trademark buckskin uniform for effect. Custer was a successful cavalry commander at both Bull Run and Gettysburg. Made a wartime brigadier general at twenty-three, he managed to be on-site to witness Lee's surrender at Appomattox.

General Custer embedded newspaper correspondents with his troops, filed monthly exploits as an Indian fighter for a published journal, and even found time to write a book. In 1874, he charged into the sacred Black Hills of South Dakota, along with gold miners, cattle, and even fascinated scientists. Despite his daring and bona fide military chops, his memorable defeat, according to most sources, was less a product of his arrogance or bad judgment than of bad timing, unreliable reconnaissance, and rudimentary battlefield communication.

Sitting Bull, *Ťhaťháŋka Íyotake* in Lakota Sioux, was a holy man, an inspirational leader, and an outspoken foe of reservation life. He and his band of Lakotas, the Hunkpapas, had refused to sign treaties or to retreat in response to increasing incursions into Indian land. Such was his eloquence and charisma, and early bravery in battles, that Sitting Bull was made chief of the Hunkpapas at the remarkable age of twenty-six and was the unprecedented selection in 1869 as supreme chief of all nontreaty bands.

He was not a large man, about five foot ten and round-shouldered with a broad chest. He walked with a slight limp due to an early bullet wound. He had a prominent nose, pronounced cheekbones, a wide mouth downturned slightly at the corners, and dark-brown eyes beneath arched eyebrows. His black hair was parted down the middle and pulled back behind his ears. Braids wrapped in fur fell to the front of his shoulders. He was said to have a "soulful look that projected no fierceness," to not have been all that consumed by combat, but in fact generous and compassionate. He was capable of sarcasm and had a dry wit and a healthy sense of humor.

After "Custer's Last Stand," the US Army, as instructed by President Grant, retaliated in earnest, sending larger-than-ever troop divisions and supplies into western Montana. Soldiers, Union and Confederate, with no Civil War to fight any longer, went west. Grant issued an ultimatum that all Sioux and Cheyenne were to be settled on reservations by the end of January 1876. Unrestrained slaughter of buffalo had begun; the goal was to deprive Indian tribes of a primary source of food in the hope that they'd become more dependent on forts and trading posts for food and provisions.

Before the Battle of Little Bighorn, Sitting Bull was already a marked man, "an obstructionist to bringing civilization to the Northern Plains buffalo grasses." Afterward, he was a wanted man. Offered a pardon, he refused to turn himself in. In 1877, after months of eluding pursuers, he and some followers escaped north into Canada. They were safe from attack—British Canada toed a fine line, not wanting to provoke a dispute with the United States—but after four years of privation, his asylum was in dire straits. His few Canadian friends, including a mounted policeman, urged him to surrender, but he held out.

Eventually, miserable weather, lack of food, and unrelenting poverty drove him back to the States, near the Missouri River, the place he knew as home. By then, he'd been abandoned by many former friends and allies. His coalition had collapsed. He found himself increasingly alone as more and more Indians saw the future and capitulated to the white man's ways, lured by much-needed handouts on reservations. Even Sitting Bull's daughter eloped and married a white man. Continuing to make war was futile.

In 1881, the Great Chief led his people back into US territory to surrender. Forty-four men and their wives and children—a ragtag group, exhausted and hungry—and their gaunt ponies, ribs showing, trudged two hundred miles south into the United States. That hot July, over the passes, down the mountains, and through the valleys, the chief led what was left of his band. They passed skeletons of buffalo killed by white men. Sitting Bull was fifty years old.

Cherie and I sat reading at a bench and table that overlooked the rolling grassy fields where the Little Bighorn River wended its way north to Hardin, Montana, and its confluence with the Bighorn River proper. We imagined seeing on the horizon a bedraggled procession walking slowly over foothills in the distance, toward Fort Buford in the Dakota Territory where Sitting Bull would give himself up.

In the lead was the tired old man, with his narrow eyes and wizened face, braided gray hair falling onto his chest. Head bowed and deep in thought about the decision he'd made, he walked alongside his pony. He'd killed so many enemies, fought so many battles his entire life. What had his valor brought him? Yes, white soldiers had fallen at Little Bighorn like "so many grasshoppers," as he'd predicted they would. But the defeat of the arrogant, yellow-haired soldier and his men had only stiffened the US government's resolve. Honored and honorable spiritual leader that he was, he made the only choice he could.

Followers trailed behind him until they reached the fort. Sitting Bull would be pardoned in exchange for his surrender, which had been arranged in advance. Even the national press was there. At 11:00 a.m. on July 20, wearing a simple bandanna pulled low, a dirty calico shirt, no adornments, and his weapon sheathed, Sitting Bull held up his hand in peace, and they let him enter. He laid down his Winchester rifle in front of the commanding officer, Major David H. Brotherton, and said, "I wish it to be remembered that I was the last man of my tribe to surrender my rifle."

The rest of the saga can be told as a combination of yet more US government duplicity, arrogance, and tragedy.

The army transferred Sitting Bull and his followers to Fort Yates in what is now North Dakota. (Today, the fort is the tribal headquarters of the Standing Rock Sioux.) Kept segregated from other Indians who were thought to be more docile, Sitting Bull's small band was moved again, to Fort Randall farther south on the Missouri River—ironically, aboard the steamboat "General Sherman." The army held Sitting Bull at Fort Randall for twenty months as a prisoner of war—not part of the surrender arrangement—before he was allowed to return to Fort Yates in 1883.

In 1884, a show promoter named Alvaren Allen of Minnesota bid for and won the right to "exhibit" Sitting Bull on a fifteen-city tour, allowed to do so by the Indian Agency for its own public relations and financial reasons. The famous and reviled "tribal chief," the "bloodthirsty savage" he most certainly was not, became a celebrity. He joined Buffalo Bill's Wild West Show. In a development almost too fanciful to be believed, he became friends with Annie Oakley. The two went on tour together. Sitting Bull became very fond of the diminutive sharpshooter, was amazed by her accuracy with firearms, and symbolically adopted her as his daughter.

What must have gone through his mind then as he rode around the arena like a trained bear, minus the collar and leash, and waved at the crowd? He brandished his weapon, and at the same time shouted curses at the onlookers in Lakota Sioux they couldn't understand. He sold pictures and autographed them. He was paid money he needed to live on, though he was known to give some away to street urchins; he couldn't understand poverty among white children. He put up with the spectacle for four months before returning to the reservation at Fort Yates.

Sitting Bull was not a model prisoner. He was restive. Can one blame him? Allowed a trip to Washington, DC, he antagonized his handlers by loudly, if eloquently, railing against more bait-and-switch legislation by Congress. Peaceful coexistence was not in his makeup. Then came the Ghost Dance movement, a faux-religious sect led by a self-proclaimed prophet, Wovoka, later called Jack Wilson. Wilson claimed to have visions, and his teachings stirred up disobedience still festering among Indians.

Sitting Bull was falsely accused of being involved in the movement, though he was not a believer. Nonetheless, the unrest suited his purposes, and surely he lent it aid and comfort. The Ghost Dance movement was never really a threat, more a form of cultural pride. But the press—including such journalistic worthies as L. Frank Baum, writing for his newspaper in Aberdeen, South Dakota Territory—seized upon it as yet another example of "confrontations" that were used by adversaries as excuses to blame Indians for disobedience, based on zero evidence. Later, Baum was to advocate for "the wholesale extirmination (sic) of the Indians … and [to] wipe these untamed and untamable creatures from the face of the earth." These days, the term is genocide.

What the Ghost Dance unrest did do was bring to fruition the long-discussed idea of arresting Sitting Bull once and for all. From the government's standpoint, he was an easy target, the symbol of the unrepentant savage. Heeding a rumor that he was going to flee the reservation, the Indian Agency for the Dakotas found its excuse. In the predawn darkness of December 15, 1890, forty-three deputized Indian Agency policemen surrounded *Tȟatȟáŋka Íyotake's* home Three of them burst in the door, awakened him, and pushed him out into the cold. They tried to get him to mount a horse. He yelled, "I will not go."

By then the commotion had drawn a crowd. The hoped-for clandestine operation wasn't going to happen. Taunts and yelling began. An enraged Lakota, an ally of Sitting Bull, fired a shot. Immediately the would-be prisoner was shot twice, including a point-blank bullet to the back of his head. Gunfire continued. Fourteen men died—eight Indians, six police.

Sitting Bull was fifty-nine. He was buried in a crude wooden coffin at Fort Yates without ceremony. Lye was poured on the dirt in an unmarked pit. Later, the Lakotas removed his body and returned it to his birthplace on the Grand River, downriver from where Cherie and I sat that day.

Today, the name Sitting Bull is usually tossed off simply as a valiant and doomed Indian leader, almost a cliché—a convenient way to acknowledge a misguided and regrettable part of our legacy. Students of history shouldn't be surprised that Sitting Bull's fame began to spread almost immediately after his death as a symbol of the Brave Noble Savage. Humans are fickle. There is now a twenty-eight-cent postage stamp with Sitting Bull's image, minted as part of the Great American series.

One hundred and forty years after Little Bighorn, Native Americans continue to fight desperate battles of a subtler sort in our "enlightened" twenty-first century. There were contemporary critics of the genocide in the nineteenth century, but they were few and ignored or ridiculed. These days, we make inadequate amends, but all too often, we just forget.

Sandwiches and two apples in our picnic basket stayed there, uneaten. We returned to the car. We had no appetite. We were overwhelmed by history.

10

Manuel Lisa

From familiar names like Sitting Bull and Custer that fill volumes and conjure up myriad images and emotions, we moved on to another name that usually elicits a "Who?" Meet Manuel Lisa.

After the Little Bighorn Battlefield, we renewed our thus-far-futile search for river confluences. Perhaps this day we would actually see with our four collective eyes an intersection of two major rivers: The Wind/Bighorn we'd been following for over 450 miles and the Yellowstone of scenic and historic fame. This time for sure, there had to be a vantage point where the two rivers merged—probably a road to the very spot and a park and stone-mounted plaque. We had high hopes.

We paralleled the Bighorn River, north to the town of Hardin, Montana, where the Little Bighorn River joins its larger sibling. Though dwarfed by the outsized reputation of the battle that bears its name, the "Little Horn" is a worthy tributary in its own right. Originating in the Bighorn Mountains near Medicine Wheel, it rambles and oxbows for 140 miles through Crow Indian land. Enough anglers seek it out to have made the river the subject of *Montana v. United States*, in which the US Supreme Court agreed that the Crow Indian Tribe had the right to regulate fishing by nontribal members.

The Yellowstone lay ahead, its headwaters in the famous park that bears its name. (Footnote: Yellowstone is the oldest national park in the US, created in 1872, four years before the battle at Little Bighorn.) Our trusty map—the paper kind you fold, not the wireless gizmo on the dash that intimidates me—told us that thirty miles past Hardin, we would find the perfectly named community of Bighorn.

Except that no such place existed, or at least we couldn't find it. Missing rivers was one thing, missing entire towns quite another. Mystified but undaunted, we came to a halt at an empty "T" intersection. There were no directions to anywhere—no sign, no building, no house or marker, and clearly no town of Bighorn.

We returned to the highway and drove a few miles east and took the next exit. A billboard announced the community of Hysham, population 312. "Montana's Hidden Treasure," founded in 1907 as a Northern Pacific Railroad siding for shipping cattle, belies its small size. We cruised past two banks, two real estate agents, two attorneys' offices, an International Harvester dealership, a butcher, baker, barber shop, hotel, pool hall, the school, the Treasure County courthouse, and, of course, a funeral home.

Impressive accomplishments by themselves these were, but pride of place went to the eye-catching Yucca Theater now on the National Register of Historic Places. A worthy description of this cinema landmark is a challenge. A large, blindingly white, two-turreted mission—vintage American Southwest— faced the street, with rows of stylish, pointy, brown log ends running along each roofline and protruding scarily out of the turrets above. In front, a covered balcony with stark-white railing posts enclosed the ground-level box office. A white sculpture of a buffalo posed on the lawn. Lewis, Clark, and Sacagawea gestured to the entrance. We didn't stop to take in a movie—*Walk Hard: The Dewey Cox Story*—nor visit the Pin-Con Confections and Ice Cream Parlor, boasting high-speed internet. Hidden treasure or no, we bade Hysham farewell and passed right through town and out on the only road there was. We had not a clue where in hell we were going.

Being lost on backroads is part of the drill on excursions we take. "Three-legged ducking" is the term passed along to me by my patient wife, courtesy of her father. He coined the phrase to make fun of travelers who explore every roadside attraction, every turnout, historic marker, or side road that "must go somewhere." These unnecessary detours, in his opinion, would only delay progress down the highway toward whatever destination the family was headed, and as such were decidedly not to be indulged on road trips in Cherie's childhood.

That's definitely not yours truly. I usually feel little guilt about poking along out into the Great Green Beyond, destination uncertain. This day, however, I wasn't so sanguine. My confidence was waning. Proud of my self-declared ability to dead reckon, we blundered along. Off to the north a dark line of trees ran in both directions. That had to mean a river, and it had to be the Yellowstone, didn't it? The distant row of foliage would approach us, then veer away, then disappear altogether as our endless little road seemed to be looping back on itself. The sky-high sun hadn't budged. Over half an hour of gallivanting out in the middle of nowhere was embarrassing my navigational skills, and we exchanged nervous looks. Wide-open Nowhere, Montana.

Then, what to our thankful eyes should finally appear around an unremarkable bend in the road? A small store and a service station, situated near the interchange before and farther west of the one we'd taken in the first place to the invisible town of Bighorn. We'd made a complete circle.

We were in Custer, Montana—tiny, but oh so welcome. A country store sat across from a highway maintenance shed and an unnamed outbuilding painted gray. Inside, a helpful young woman in a calico apron explained to us the error of our byways. It seems that up a side road paralleling the highway for a short distance was the town of Bighorn after all. We frowned but kept our mouths shut.

"But it's not there," she said patiently. She continued in the familiar argot of a friendly local giving a clueless traveler advice. (E.g., "Don't turn at the first tree. Turn at the second; no, not the one by the big rock, et cetera.")

She went on. "Bighorn's actually across a bridge, and it's not really a town, just a couple of buildings where Somebody-or-Other has his ranch."

That certainly cleared things up. A Diet Coke and an energy bar later, we followed her directions and ended up at the very same Bighorn exit as before, at the "T." We turned right, crossed the bridge, and found nothing, as she'd told us we would. Where was the river, or the confluence, or anything, for that matter?

"Nothing but a fence and a field," I groaned.

But wait! I'd spoken too soon. Back before we'd crossed the bridge to non-Bighorn, I'd gotten a quick glance at a sign that had on it the diagram of a red fish eyeing a hook, the logo of the Montana Fish, Wildlife & Parks Department. The sign said, MANUEL LISA PUBLIC FISHING ACCESS. Whoa! We reversed course and pulled into a small, dirt parking lot. But how unfair I knew this to be.

As every vehicular traveler knows, roadside markers never fail to point out this or that tidbit of local, often forgettable information. Mile after highway mile, blue or brown or green signs urge the tourist to stop at an upcoming gravel turnout and read the notice nailed to a weathered four-by-four or on a tarnished metal plaque anchored in a granite obelisk. Once in a while, the information is noteworthy—LEWIS AND CLARK CAMPED ALONG THIS CREEK IN 1805 or GEORGE WASHINGTON SLEPT HERE.

Often as not, though, the minutiae are laughable. A homemade sign in the middle of Anytown will advise the voyager to stop and honor the birthplace of Ralph Waldo McGillicuddy, noted inventor of the two-handled screwdriver and later the foot-pedal-operated butter churn. We once saw a decorative sign at the crossroads of a tiny town that pointed to a park, one block square, with a perfectly manicured lawn and picnic tables beneath swaying sycamore trees. The town fathers and mothers had dedicated the green space to the memory of

Favorite Daughter Trinity Cather, second cousin by marriage, once removed, of the author Willa, and one-time mayor.

Birders might be interested to know that we once passed the last-known nesting site of the rare Southern California clapper rail—in Wyoming. An Audubon Society sign said so. Our favorite this trip: Montana High Desert Petting Zoo. Beneath the title was the outline of a coiled snake, fangs presented, and the words Tortoise, Gila Monster, Jackrabbit, Rattler—at least two of which critters were no nearer Montana than miles to the southwest. You get the idea. Don't even get me started on billboards. (E.g., See Rock City, Wall Drug, Little America, Mystery Spot, South of the Border.)

So how hard would it be to mark river junctions? Big, important rivers?

We bumped across ruts into the dusty lot and parked in the shade. Here, the last reach of the Bighorn River sauntered north. Two fishermen, a boy and his dad, waded through the reeds into the shallows. A posted notice warned canoeists about strong currents up the way at the Yellowstone River, out of sight, but we were fresh out of canoes.

Adding insult to injury, at this forgettable spot was an unforgivably inadequate tribute to one Manuel Lisa.

I leaned my forehead against the steering wheel. Cherie rubbed my shoulders.

"This is wrong," I said. "So wrong."

"I know you're disappointed."

"Just wrong," I repeated.

"About not finding where the rivers meet. I agree."

"Not that. Manuel Lisa."

"What about him?"

I sighed. "All the other mountain men of the West are honored everywhere. Colter, Bridger, Carson, Jed Smith. Manuel Lisa could've bought and sold all of them. In fact, he employed two of them. And this is what he gets? A crummy fishing hole?"

Jim Bridger and Jedediah Smith have entire national forests named after them. Kit Carson, brutal slayer of Apaches, has a namesake state capital of Nevada and a US highway mountain pass over the Sierra Nevadas. Dime novels were written about him. John Jacob Astor founded Astoria on the Oregon Coast.

People know about John Colter, if only for his famously scary, buck-nekkid scamper through the woods for miles with angry Blackfeet on his tail. But he was also a member of the Lewis and Clark Expedition and the first European to see Yellowstone. An area of sulfurous springs and steamy geysers is still called "Colter's Hell."

We got out of the car and soaked a towel with ice water from the cooler. Trading it back and forth for our hot foreheads, I continued my unasked-for biography.

Granted, the name Manuel Lisa does not lightly trip off the tongue. But at a time when it was anybody's guess who would control the lucrative fur trade in western North America, let alone the western continent itself, Lisa was among the first to distinguish himself. He and his men broke paths and paddled up rivers and traded with Indians throughout the Louisiana Territory.

"He established a trading post near this very spot in 1807!" I waved my arm around. "Here! Called it Fort Raymond after his son. People also called it Fort Manuel. Now, just trees and brush, two fishermen, mosquitoes, and a sluggish river."

Originally a Spanish citizen born in New Orleans, Manuel Lisa became a successful man of commerce in St. Louis. He formed the Missouri Fur Company along with William Clark of expedition fame and the Choteau brothers, among others. He built Fort Raymond, then in 1809 abandoned it because of hostile Indians and founded a new outpost on the Little Missouri River in western North Dakota. He named that outpost Fort Lisa—aka another Fort Manuel. According to some accounts, Sacagawea died at Fort Lisa in 1812 and was buried there. She was twenty-four.

During the War of 1812, Manuel Lisa took the lead in

negotiating with friendly tribes against those allied with the British. The latter repaid him by burning down the second Fort Lisa in 1813. Today, the site cannot be visited since it's far beneath the surface of the lake now named Sakakawea.

Pioneering and fur-trading expeditions to the West continued after the war. All a frontiersman needed was a carbine and a little cornmeal in a sack, as the saying went. Mountain men, seasoned trappers, and malcontents swarmed the Rockies, many of them employees of Manuel Lisa. He stayed in the game, made plenty of money, built a fine house, and entertained well. His last venture was into Nebraska where he founded yet another Fort Lisa near what is now Omaha. He is credited with being the first permanent US settler in that territory, where he continued to establish friendly, albeit lucrative, alliances with Native American tribes as an official Indian agent. His Missouri Fur Company was a prime competitor of Astor's American Fur Company, and later, Bridger and Smith's Rocky Mountain Fur Company. Astor soon monopolized the trade, but by the time of Lisa's death in 1820, the once-prosperous fur trade was near its end.

So, too, was our friend the Bighorn River, tantalizingly close enough to its confluence with the Yellowstone that we could smell it. Disappointing? No more than the lame footnote, the Manuel Lisa Public Fishing Access, courtesy of the Great State of Montana. A fishing hole. Now, maybe if he'd *invented* something … like a two-handled screwdriver or a better butter churn …

That day, we managed to cool off in the shade, leaning against the car and brushing away flurries of cottonwood seeds dancing in a light breeze.

"Another wild grouse chase," I quipped.

"Two, actually, if you count your amigo, Señor Lisa," Cherie replied.

We got back in the car and left, tires spinning in the dust just a little bit. We pushed on to the Missouri River, less than hopeful, it must be said.

11

The Missouri!

After bidding a tearful farewell to Manuel Lisa and the nonexistent community of Bighorn, we endured 150 miles of Interstate 94 East, which again pretty much followed the Lewis & Clark National Historic Trail. The Yellowstone River continued to keep us company behind a distant line of trees to the north. Our objective was a visit to Fort Union and Fort Buford the next day, both fateful outposts about a mile from each other near where the Yellowstone meets the mighty Missouri River. Would our "rivers confluence" bad luck continue even at that notable junction?

We spent the night in Miles City, Montana. The town of eight thousand is named for General Nelson A. Miles, who founded a stockade there after the battle at Little Bighorn to control remaining "uncontrolled" Indians. (Miles reportedly said, however, that "whiskey caused him more trouble than the Indians," so he threw its purveyors out of town.) In time, the city became a major livestock railhead. In fact, I first heard the name Miles City as a destination for Gus and Call's cattle drive in *Lonesome Dove*, a story so memorably told by Larry McMurtry that I was teary-eyed when the book ended. Our time in Miles was brief and uneventful. Perhaps we shouldn't have missed the annual Bucking Horse Sale two weeks earlier.

The great, storied river of the northern Rockies, the Yellowstone—the *Roche jaune* or *Piere jaune* (sic)—is the largest tributary by volume of water that Lewis and Clark and the Corps of Discovery confronted on their expedition up the Missouri. Meriwether Lewis described the scene from a nearby hilltop where the Yellowstone met the Missouri as "a most pleasing view of the country, perticularly of the wide and fertile vallies formed by [the two rivers]."

Fort Union was built in 1828, not so much a fort as a trading post, a suitable place for boats to unload and reload. The outpost served as the western base for John Jacob Astor's American Fur Company, which by then had a monopoly on the trade. Fort Union became the most important fur-trading post in the West until after the Civil War. Since it exactly straddles the Montana–North Dakota border, the day of our visit, we unwittingly wandered back and forth between Mountain and Central time zones—without changing our watches.

Remarkably, for nearly forty years Fort Union maintained harmonious relations with neighboring Indian tribes. Residents and travelers, even some from Europe, mingled with one another and with natives. The fur trade eventually collapsed due, among other things, to the growing scarcity of furs and the changing style in hats. (Silk had become the fashion.) In time, the *bourgeois*, the man in charge of the fort, ordered even the post's eclectically provisioned kitchen to be demolished and the wood used for steamboat fuel. The entire fort was dismantled in 1867.

Today, an imposing, full-scale reconstruction stands on a rise above the North Dakota countryside—a solid, very tall wooden enclosure of bright-white fencing, rebuilt to exact specifications. On two corners, tall guardhouses called "bastions" stand vigil, with portholes cut in them for cannon and rifles. We walked to the front gate, put a shoulder to the heavy wooden doorway, and entered. Facing us was a central flagpole, and past it, the fort headquarters, a bright orange-roofed, two-story structure with a porch in front and a lookout and bell tower on the roof. There were outlines at our feet made of rough-hewn timbers that marked where a storage house or lodging had been, an icehouse, and a blacksmith shop or the powder magazine. The eighteen-foot-high, white fence encloses

the entire fort interior and has a walkway running around the
perimeter, a defensive palisade.

We had the place to ourselves. We listened to the high walls
whose predecessors once knew French, Cherokee, German, Sioux,
or frontier English. The peaceful camaraderie at Fort Union
came to an end as the Indian Wars picked up in the 1860s.

Inside the modest visitor center we questioned the
informative young docent about the deterioration of friendly
relations between tribes and white men. He remarked,
"Everything's fine until the government gets involved." (I chose
not to bore him with my sermon about ordinary citizens such
as we who hope to just get along, raise kids, coach soccer, take
vacations. The older I get, and the more I travel the country, the
more my Libertarian streak grows.) We gave the young man a
nice tip, acknowledging wisdom beyond his years, then took the
short road to nearby Fort Buford.

Buford was constructed in 1866, make no mistake about
it, to serve as a military post—to be a stronghold from which to
protect immigrants making the journey west. Unlike Fort Union,
Fort Buford has not been restored. A small structure on the
actual site now only serves as an information center. We skipped
it, doubting that our experience would be significantly enhanced
by going into the plain-looking building with maps on the wall.
We doubted we'd learn much more on the subject of the Indian
Wars, settler invasions, US perfidy—the whole sad mess.

However, what happened next, when we rounded a
bend in the road moments later, was like finding gold. There,
smack in front of us, was the Mother of All Sought-After River
Confluences, the Yellowstone joining the Missouri before our
very eyes. High-fives and grins. We hadn't been on a fool's
errand for fifteen hundred miles.

And there was no measly little roadside sign or cutesy park,
but a worthy commemoration of a geologic and geographic and
historic treasure. The interpretive center was in a large, modern
facility with attendants at the ready and a movie theater to

boot. Outside, past the building and beyond the tall grass, was the Missouri River itself, drifting in from the west, slow and placid. Directly across from where we stood and gaped, the Yellowstone came straight toward us from the south, likewise broad and unhurried.

We high-fived again and planted ourselves on a picnic table bench beneath the rustle of ubiquitous cottonwood trees. The musty scent of the marsh below wafted up from the bluff. As if on cue, an osprey hovered in a diamond-blue sky as if it had been painted there on a canvas by Albert Bierstadt. I stood and walked to the bluff's edge.

That's when I saw it—in the distance, coming up the Yellowstone toward me, a Ping-Pong ball. *The* Ping-Pong ball.

"Cherie," I yelled. "Come quick!"

"Oh my God, what?" she said, running over from the table where she'd been decanting ice water from the thermos.

"Look!"

"At what?" I think I'd frightened her.

I pointed. "Out there. That little speck of white coming toward us, bobbing in the current. Don't you see? Between those ripples."

She squinted in the direction I pointed to.

"Nope."

"It's the Ping-Pong ball!"

She gently took my arm. "Honey, come back over here and sit down."

"But it's out there." By then, though, I'd lost it among the whitecaps.

"I'm sure you saw it. Now, you need to get out of the sun."

"But …" I protested.

"We decided not to do the Ping-Pong ball thing. Remember?"

"Oh." She had me there. "But it might have made it."

"It certainly might have. Here, have a sip."

I wiped away a tear. Maybe something got in my eye. We walked back to the table. I took a couple of glances over my shoulder.

Mirages are common in the West, or anywhere that imagination encounters heat waves shimmering in the distance. Sometimes they're ripples off the asphalt on the road ahead, sometimes they conjure up things that aren't there, like thirsty stragglers in the Sahara seeing waving palm trees in the distance. If someone can see water in a desert, what's so odd about seeing a Ping-Pong ball floating along a body of water?

12

Corps of Discoverers

Bernard DeVoto, in the third book of his trilogy on the exploration of the American West, *The Course of Empire*, wrote:

> the Missouri River: swift, hurling its matted
> debris at any craft that entered it, perilous with
> snags and boils and sandbars and crumbling
> banks, the channels to be found only as they
> were come upon and always changing.

The peaceful meandering of the Missouri we watched from our perch on the bluff that day was a far cry from its turbulent past. Sticks and branches floated downstream in no hurry at all, drifting and spinning near the shore. Not for a moment, however, will I gainsay the excitement, the goose bumps on my skin, taking it all in, Ping-Pong ball or not.

With the temperature continuing to climb, it was impossible not to think of Lewis and Clark and their epic journey. How naive our young nation was a mere year after the Louisiana Purchase in 1803 when the Corps of Discovery followed its leaders into parts unknown. The nineteenth century was still in its infancy; a mere twenty-five years had elapsed since the signing of the Declaration of Independence, and only fourteen since George Washington took the oath of office. Maps of the day were either exaggerated or based on myth or rumor, and pretty much useless. The Northwest Passage was thought to exist; so, too, the fabled cities of gold in the Southwest and the nonexistent Strait of Anian, located either north of, or south of, someplace called "the Californias." No one was sure.

The easygoing Missouri River headwaters begin where three modest rivers converge four thousand feet up in the central Rockies. Christened by Lewis and Clark after Thomas Jefferson, Treasury Secretary Albert Gallatin, and James Madison, the three tributaries intersect in Missouri Headwaters State Park near the town of Three Forks, Montana. On an earlier visit there, Cherie and I watched a solitary beaver paddle toward us, barely making ripples in the stream. The blue water that quietly murmured along in front of where we stood on its gravel shore gave not a hint of what was to come—not a clue that, over the next twenty-three hundred miles, tributary after tributary would join the river. The Platte, Kansas, Milk, James, White, Niobara, Little Missouri, Osage, Big Sioux, and of course the Yellowstone, along with others, together drain half a million square miles of watershed.

In the sixteenth and seventeenth centuries, England, Spain, and France vied with each another, racing for territory in the New World. While Martin Luther was busy nailing ninety-five theses to a church door, Leonardo was painting the Mona Lisa, and Copernicus was reimagining the universe, European explorers on the new continent were leapfrogging one another, tracking, trapping, and conquering natives farther and farther into Canada and the American West on behalf of their gold- and fur-hungry sponsors. They'd all heard rumors of a big river that rose in the West and crossed the continent—wishful thinking, for the most part. But discovery of the Missouri River eluded explorers for over a century and a half.

Hernando De Soto was the first Spanish seeker of fabled riches in the New World. In 1541, he ventured up the Mississippi—his *Rio del Espíritu Santo*—over six hundred miles from the Gulf of Mexico, pushing tantalizingly close to the junction with the Missouri before turning back. In the same year, Francisco Coronado led his troops throughout the desert Southwest, heads full of visions of palace rooms

nine feet deep in gold [and] Indian corn in
which the golden ear was sheathed in broad
leaves of silver from which hung a rich tassel of
threads of the same precious metal.
(Bernard DeVoto)

Instead of the fabled Seven Golden Cities of Cíbola, the
conquistadors found rudimentary Indian villages—adobe walls,
thatched roofs, subsistence farming—but also heard stories
about a big river flowing out of mountains in the northwest.
Too exhausted and frustrated to chase hearsay, Coronado gave
up and returned to Mexico.

Explorers and chroniclers of the day had no conception of
the Rocky Mountains or the extent of the continent. As far as
they knew, rivers coming out of the west originated in India.
Their innocence is understandable. Latitude—positions on the
globe north and south—could be roughly calculated by sun
risings and settings and by tracking stars at night. Longitude
was another matter. Measuring distances east and west had to
await development of an accurate chronometer, a timepiece. A
reasonably reliable one was not invented until the middle of
the eighteenth century. Dead reckoning had to suffice in the
meantime.

According to DeVoto, the French of Louis XIV were the
most successful of explorers in the New World. During the Sun
King's seventy-two-year reign and that of his successor, Louis XV,
France consolidated its hold throughout upstate New York, on
and around the Great Lakes, and eventually to the Mississippi.
By contrast, English colonists on the Atlantic seaboard and
the Spanish in the southwest and Florida could not compete.
The French were better skilled in negotiating with the many
capricious and wary Indian tribes—Huron, Ottowa, Miami,
Mohawk, Illinois, Erie, Chippewa, Assiniboine, Fox, and the
most warlike and feared of them all, the Iroquois. From Europe
they brought fascinating products to trade with the *sauvages* like

cotton cloth and blankets, objects made of metal, such as pots and pans, and eventually weapons. In return, furs, not gold, were sent back to France.

By the early seventeenth century, for context, Sir Walter Raleigh had lost a colony in Roanoke, and Galileo Galilei had found the moons of Jupiter. Charles I of England had recently lost his head. It was persevering French frontiersmen who eventually did locate the rumored great river flowing into the Mississippi from the west.

Explorer Louis Jolliet and Jesuit father Jacques Marquette and their party loaded birchbark canoes and set off along an ancient Indian route westward from Lake Michigan. They paddled down the Wisconsin River and then the Mississippi. Near the end of June, 1673, Father Marquette wrote that they

> heard the noise of a rapid, into which we
> were about to run. I have seen nothing more
> dreadful. An accumulation of large and entire
> trees, branches, and floating islands was
> issuing from the mouth of the Pekistanoui
> [Missouri] with such impetuosity that we could
> not without great danger risk passing through
> it. (DeVoto)

The water was chocolate-brown, noisy, boiling at them, logs twirling like tops. Mist curtained off everything except the mouth. But Jolliet and Marquette had not found the fabled waterway everyone assumed led west to the Pacific Ocean.

Lewis and Clark were to take the river's measure in 1804 ... 130 years later.

Montana is a big state, a very big state. It is larger than Germany or Italy; the entire United Kingdom would fit inside Montana with room to spare. A big state, but empty for the most part. Twice as many people live in incorporated King

County, Washington, the home of Seattle, than in all of
Montana. The story is told that a trio of Corps explorers, after
months of travel up the Missouri and beyond, summited a ridge
in what is now Western Montana near the Continental Divide.
They gazed out to the west, expecting to see the Pacific Ocean
beyond. What they saw instead were ranges of dark mountain
peaks extending to the far horizon. They still had a thousand
miles to go.

Until the construction of dams in the twentieth century, the
size and brawn of the Missouri was no exaggeration. Lewis and
Clark's men had poled and pulled their cumbersome boats—a
fifty-five-foot keelboat and two pirogues, smaller flat-bottom
craft—from St. Louis to the Yellowstone.

The Great Falls of the Missouri interrupted the river in
mid-Montana, five successive waterfalls that rumble and roar
for twenty-one miles above and below what is now the city of
Great Falls. The Corps of Discovery could hear them thunder
well before they got to them. The largest was eighty feet high.
Portage was the only option, so the Corps built two dugout
canoes to use as sledges and attached ropes with which to pull
them.

Cherie and I got a taste of the physical challenge required
when we stopped at the Lewis and Clark Interpretive Center
near Great Falls on a previous trip. We experienced, literally
hands-on, the power of the Missouri River back in the day.
Curators had rigged up a tempting exhibit, a full-sized wooden
boat poised on boulders and inclined down to a mezzanine
below. With thick, sturdy ropes hanging from its bow, visitors
were invited to pull on the ropes to test their strength against
the "current." Could they move the boat?

How could I resist? The rope was made of twisted brown
twine as thick as my wrist. I grasped it with my decidedly
uncalloused hands, planted my feet, and tugged. Nothing. I
leaned back and strained. Not a budge, not an inch. I strung

the rope over my shoulder, turned around, bent my legs, and pulled like hell. Cherie helped. My hands hurt. I dropped the stupid rope. I looked around. Fortunately the place was nearly empty, and there were no onlookers … other than a courteous attendant who stifled a grin. He'd seen it all before.

We tried to imagine the struggle. Even without waterfalls, the men of the Corps accomplished only ten or fifteen miles on a good day. Hordes of insects menaced them with each step. Rattlesnakes were around. Meriwether Lewis faced off against a grizzly bear. The heat was intense, and prickly pear cactus chewed up moccasins. The shifting river's current always pushed against them. It took the party a month to portage over and around the five great falls. We wondered again and again how they did any of it, those forty-five stalwart adventurers— never sure they were on the right path and with no idea how far they had yet to go. In Stephen Ambrose's word, they were "undaunted."

Lewis wrote of the torrent of water in front of him, "the grandest sight":

> [F]rom the reflection of the sun on the sprey
> or mist which arrises from these falls is a
> beautifull rainbow produced which adds not
> little to the beauty of this majestically grand
> senery (sic).

In Lewis and Clark's wake, other explorers followed. They wasted little time accepting the challenge of the big river, hand-rowing or paddling or pulling boats. They braved the shifting sandbars, rain torrents, snags, and floating logs and deadheads, not to mention angry Indians. Steamboats eventually did the same, but only took on the river in low water during late summer or during spring floods. Today, all but one of the Great Falls is submerged. Pacified by fifteen dams, much of the mighty river is a now a chain of reservoirs. As some consolation,

149 miles of the upper Missouri, downriver of Great Falls, still runs free through the Upper Missouri River Breaks, one of the nation's Wild and Scenic Rivers.

The panorama from the bluff where we sat by Fort Buford was anything but turbulent. No swirling eddies, heavy currents, or scary rapids. Just quiet, two big rivers lazing along, hedged by fields and riparian trees and shrubs, unspectacular certainly to a casual observer. Nothing remarkable, I suppose. Except to us.

Was it anticlimactic? Not a bit. The Missouri and Yellowstone Rivers pack enough history to crowd a library, several libraries full of books. How many thousands and thousands of years have these rivers run? How many mere mortals like us, who measure out our lives with coffee spoons, have vied and strived along their banks and left their legacy?

We were in no hurry to leave. But after a while, with a sigh, we returned to the car and set off for North Dakota.

13

SimCity

We crossed into the new time zone in North Dakota, and were soon in a different reality as well. A few miles after our reverie at the Yellowstone and Missouri River confluence, it was as if we'd passed through the looking glass and found ourselves in the middle of a popular computer game—"SimCity." In fact, this was Williston, North Dakota, smack in the heart of Bakken oil country.

"Frackin' Chicken" on the menu should have tipped us off. We feigned nonchalance and studied our choices while the server at a Doc Holliday's restaurant awaited our order, her foot tapping, pad in hand. I chose the burger, and Cherie, fish and chips.

We had left Forts Union and Buford behind, continuing to track the Missouri River. The river would soon reach its northernmost point in the US at Williston, only sixty miles south of the Canadian border. The long northern arc of the river was the only route Lewis and Clark could be sure of in 1803—a far greater distance than the more direct routes into the Rockies discovered later. Surely the corpsmen were relieved when the river finally began curving toward southern latitudes just to the west.

For a while the scenery was postcard perfect. With the car windows down and enjoying somewhat cooler temps, we drove along spacious green fields typical of the Northern Plains. Farmhouses with long driveways lined with cottonwoods stood guard over fields of neatly rolled cylinders of hay. Groves of trees decorated an endless backdrop of sprawling countryside. Cows and calves and horses and colts grazed beneath a crystal-clear dome of blue sky. Certainly, nothing would possibly interrupt the scene, as idyllic as a landscape by Constable. Nothing … or so we thought.

Had Sitting Bull on his journey home crested a hill a few miles east of Fort Buford today, he would have stopped in his tracks and stared off in the distance at an *ostrich* bobbing its head down to the ground and back up. It's possible he had heard white men speak of such an exotic species of fowl, but not on the Northern Plains. As he drew closer, before him would stand a mechanical, man-made oddity beyond even his intelligent imagination—or that of his nineteenth-century US Army foes, for that matter. (Curious note: There is paleontological evidence that ostriches did in fact stroll the North American continent in Jurassic times.)

We were caught up short, too, and slowed down. In someone's front yard stood a spanking-clean horsehead pump, dipping down and up, down and up. It looked brand new. A storage tank beside the house was painted pastel blue. Nodding slowly, this sate-of-the-art contrivance looked nothing like the ugly prototypes I'd seen as a kid when the family drove down Highway 99 through the California Central Valley.

Farther down the highway, we saw them everywhere, pumps and color-coordinated round repositories on front lawns, back yards, lots next door—marigold orange, chiffon yellow, mint green.

As a youngster, I'd often wondered whether anyone besides me had ever noticed that the outsized head of an oil pumpjack looked remarkably like a Tyrannosaurus rex bending down to take a drink, then looking back up for the odd hadrosaur to snack on. Is it too much of a gruesome stretch to imagine that the mechanical look-alikes today are sipping the oily, decomposed, and squished bodies of millions upon millions of their long-ago relatives? Innocent and ignorant, tall as trees and big as houses, dinosaurs roamed the continents and seas of the Carboniferous Era until a meteorological shift betrayed them. We, their successors, not so ignorant nor innocent, betray ourselves, rush hour by rush hour.

The town of Williston in the northwestern corner of North

Dakota is the epicenter of Bakken oil country. The community and its surrounds epitomize the hold that the oil industry has on the state. The Bakken Formation is one of the largest—and now infamous—contiguous deposits of oil and natural gas in the United States, occupying close to 20 percent of North Dakota and extending into Montana and Canada.

Good old Farmer Bakken. What hath he wrought? Henry Bakken was the son of Norwegian immigrants, and the old homestead was pretty quiet until 1951 when the first oil well came in, drilled by the Amerada Petroleum Company. Bakken's namesake legacy now consists of a Who's Who of industry giants, and their enormous footprints abound. The mechanics of extraction from deep in the shale and dolomite deposits are everywhere. The plumbing, processing, and transporting support a thriving economy.

So it was that the computer game SimCity came to mind on the road to Williston and beyond on hills and on flatlands extending over five hundred square miles. On dirt-cleared empty lots and well pads, and along pipeline corridors, structures looked like they'd been placed there by extraterrestrial gamers. We imagined giant children in an alternate universe, creating commercial or residential zones and parks and trails with a keystroke or mouse-click: "Let's see, I'll place a store here, a gas station there, and some trees. Density, budget? Hmmm, a road to apartments over there, next to a what? Oh, gotta leave room for the *oil wells*."

Intact rows of six-unit apartments might well have come off an assembly line—picked up at a construction yard, loaded onto an eighteen-wheeler, then plopped down on a convenient plot. Nursery-grown trees anchored by burlapped root balls leaned against buildings next to idling backhoes. We passed a four-story, bland brown-and-beige bandbox, a "high rise," advertising "Rooms - $79.95." One upscale subdivision was gated, no less, with an ornate arch over a newly paved entrance.

A mile or so of wide-open prairie was followed by more

construction equipment: Dozers and graders, fresh off a Caterpillar or Komatsu lot. Smelly asphalt machines and clanking shovels and backed-up dump trucks negotiated lines of orange cones and flaggers with hard hats. There were carwashes, too, antidotes for the fine dust that lingered everywhere. A junkyard full of rusting automobile hulks sat alongside a used-car lot with "one-owner" RVs. As one oil patch plays out, it seems workers are relocated and their barracks deserted.

The trade-off? In nearby Watford City, the streets were newly paved, with bicycle lanes, and flower baskets hung from ornate light standards. Main Street was lined with colorful shop fronts. We saw a bright, new high school, a restored theater, a library with a new façade. The city park had been spiffed up with new swings and safety-approved playground equipment.

Cherie and I did not rush to judgment, however. What we witnessed in Bakken country was uncomfortable, like those photographs they showed in school of what cigarettes do to your lungs. We decided not to blithely gainsay the thriving economy in an otherwise subsistence-level corner of America. It felt a little too facile for card-carrying environmentalists from the pristine Pacific Northwest to lambaste unbridled oil extraction.

For instance, I recorded what we saw on a bright-red Moleskine notebook, a freebie courtesy of a left-leaning *New York Review of Books* subscription. We rode along in an automobile that inhaled and exhaled. The Pacific Northwest's silver, skyscraping cities and Microsoft/Amazon culture belie a legacy of mountain-skinning logging, depleted—and frequently quarantined—shellfish beds, and strict limits on iconic Dungeness crab. Protecting and restoring once-robust salmon runs has only recently become a state priority. Removal of unneeded dams is finally beginning. Nor can I ignore the fact that four of the five Washington State oil refineries are within the sound of my muffler, in our county and the one next-door. A coalition of local native tribes plus environmentalists barely

defeated, for the present, an attempt to site what would have
been the largest coal-shipping terminal on the West Coast.

Begun in 2000, fracking is a relatively recent phenomenon,
and the "sweet," low-sulfur, if high-risk product it extracts
is worth a lot of money. In 2013, North Dakota, second only
to Texas in domestic oil production, enjoyed a $1 billion
budget surplus. Times are a-changing, however. The "frenzied
prosperity"—as *Scientific American* dubbed it in 2012—in North
Dakota is slowing down. A decline in crop prices nationwide
and the undercutting of oil prices by Middle East producers
combined to gouge a $300 million hole in the state budget. It
is unclear what the impact will be on the construction and
earth-moving industries we saw, not to mention schools and
housing. But in Williston and the Bakken oil basin, business
was booming.

So go ahead, Willistonians, and have a little fun nicknaming
a menu item after an explosive. Speaking of food, I was
getting hungry, even homesick. I looked forward to being in
my backyard with some guests on one of our long Northwest
summer evenings and cooking on my barbecue. I'd spread a
little chopped garlic and basil onto a chunk of king salmon,
aka Chinook, and throw it on the Weber. As far as I know, at
home in Washington is the only place in the United States
where a guy can fire up the barby and legally treat his guests
to an entrée that is classified in some places as a threatened or
endangered species by the US Fish and Wildlife Service.
It's delicious, and goes great with spotted owl drumettes.

14

Teddy Roosevelt

We had a decision to make before morning. The section of the Missouri River we might follow next was in fact a reservoir, the seventy miles of Lake Sakakawea, the longest of fifteen man-made lakes on the Big Muddy. Thirty-five percent of the river today consists of a chain of reservoirs. The next confluence would be the mightiest, that with the Mississippi, over a thousand miles away.

Sakakawea Lake is, of course, generously named for Lewis and Clark's Shoshone guide, scout, negotiator, translator … and friend, one hopes. The thoughtful gesture stops there. The lake is contained behind Garrison Dam, named for army troops stationed near there to keep the peace—i.e., subdue mischievous Indians. Moreover, construction of Garrison, the fifth-largest earthen dam in the world, by the US Army Corps of Engineers between 1947 and 1953, succeeded in forcibly dislocating one thousand seven hundred Native Americans and destroyed the way of life of countless others who for millennia depended on the river. Forced to accept $5 million as remuneration for reservation land taken, the Three Affiliated Tribes—Mandan, Hidatsa, and Arikara—were, to add insult to injury, prohibited from fishing, grazing, and hunting along the shoreline. But it was not for that reprehensible, if not unprecedented, factoid that we changed our plans.

At Williston, we'd gained another perspective, a different slice of America—sociologic and economic—unlike others on our trip to that point. Plus, we were on a cusp, so to speak; on the border between historic pioneering into unknown mountains, up nameless creeks, and into gaping valleys. Next would come the largely agrarian settlement in the flatlands beyond to the east.

The big sluggish Missouri ahead would veer down through South Dakota, then Iowa, then Omaha and Kansas City, before turning east again across Missouri to St. Louis, home of the Gateway Arch. True, if we stayed the riverine course, we could take in Jones-Confluence Point State Park outside of St. Louis, surely the granddaddy of all confluences. Though without the unbridled turbulence Fr. Marquette and Louis Joliet saw, that joining of waters would be something to behold.

We still held in our thoughts the "cup of water" we imagined flowing past us in Jakey's Fork high in the Rockies at Union Pass. Chasing along rivers out of the mountains and into the plains had taught us so much more than hydraulics. But we hadn't, from the outset, contemplated going all the way to New Orleans and the Gulf. Another day, perhaps. So, with apologies to Plains States folks and a goodbye to Jakey's Fork and successors, we left the Missouri River and drove south. Fracking and pumpjacking and flaggers in hard hats behind us, the landscape opened up and glorious scenery took over.

The Theodore Roosevelt Expressway, or "TRE" in local parlance, is a part of US Highway 85 that passes through Williston, then on south toward Medora, South Dakota. (Highway 85 begins at the border with Canada and runs fifteen hundred miles to Texas and Mexico.) Traffic was light to nonexistent on yet another sun-filled morning.

Along the way, we stopped at the Little Missouri State Park, an out-of-the-way camping site and facility for packhorses. With a quiet crunch of gravel, we coasted to a stop. Four-footed hirelings nickered in the background, and white-crowned sparrows hopped around, pretending to be hungry. Across a grassy common behind us, a motor home's door snicked shut. The smiling camp host gave us a wave and a "howdy" and set off for his tractor. He and it clattered away, and we had the place to ourselves. We stood by a split-rail fence, binoculars sweeping the distance, and contemplated the landscape of yet another remarkable, if less-storied river, the Little Missouri. We caught glimpses of the far-off river where it skirted intervening hills. The silence was cleansing.

The Little Missouri River rises in northeastern Wyoming, west of Devil's Tower of *Close Encounters* fame. Quiet and placid for 560 miles, the river meanders across a corner of southeast Montana and into South Dakota. An important marker of the Northern Plains in its own right, it's the river that nourishes the popular Badlands National Park. From there the river northward crosses the Little Missouri National Grassland, a million acres of protected prairie, the largest in the United States. The Little Missouri joins its bigger sibling and the two rivers form an arm of a reservoir on Lake Sakakawea where a bay now covers one of Manuel Lisa's forts.

Sunlight prickling through pine and oak trees reminded us we had to move along. Souls and bodies refreshed and coffee mugs replenished, we set off. Our upcoming destination was Theodore Roosevelt National Park, a storied destination not to be missed. It was altogether fitting and proper that we stopped there: the year 2016 marked the centennial of the National Parks System, "America's best idea," according to Wallace Stegner. Teddy Roosevelt said, "I never would have been President if it had not been for my experiences in North Dakota."

In 1884, the twenty-five-year-old Harvard graduate, scion of a well-to-do family and a rising star in New York politics, suffered the loss of both his wife Alice and his mother Martha on the very same day. He abandoned public life and escaped to the rugged North Dakota outdoors which he'd visited before, fishing and hunting bison. TR's interest in all things natural had begun in childhood as a sickly youngster. In the Dakota wilderness, grief-stricken, he healed and he wrote. His commitment to the conservation ethic grew, and eventually he returned to serve his country in ways that are enshrined.

From time to time, Roosevelt returned to North Dakota

where he founded two ranches and raised cattle in the hills. A cabin and a ranch house still stand. As a protoenvironmentalist, during his presidency he created the US Forest Service. Largely through his efforts and those of others, John Muir and Gifford Pinchot for example, in 1916 President Wilson signed the National Park Service Organic Act. Hence, the national park in western North Dakota that bears Roosevelt's name.

Teddy Roosevelt even had a thing about rivers. Compared to presidents who followed him, TR continued to be a wide-eyed adventurer and global thinker. He never stopped exploring. Consistent with his lifelong vigorous lifestyle—and after his ten-year presidency, after the Bull Moose political schism in his own party, after an assassination attempt, and after Woodrow Wilson defeated him in a landslide in 1912—Roosevelt set off to South America with his son Kermit on an expedition to find the headwaters of the "River of Doubt" in Brazil. The adventure through the Amazon jungle was nearly fatal, with all the pitfalls and injuries and sickness one might expect for travel on a completely uncharted river for over six hundred miles. At one point Roosevelt suffered an infection that made it impossible for him to walk for days. The expedition was gone more than seven months, and could not communicate with the outside world, before returning home safe and sound. TR never stopped talking about it.

He died in his sleep in 1919 at Sagamore Hill, his primary residence that overlooked the water of Oyster Bay, Long Island. He was sixty-one. One mourner, Thomas Marshall, Woodrow Wilson's Vice President, said, "had he been awake, there would have been a fight."

We picked up a map at the ranger station and set off on the thirty-six-mile Scenic Loop Drive through the Southern Unit of the Park. The celebrated resident bison seemed to be elsewhere that day—shades of bighorn sheep, it occurred to us—but we didn't take it personally. The iconic herbivores are said to be more plentiful in the smaller North Unit of the park that we did not visit.

There was nothing superficial or artificial about the "TR." No out-of-place distractions. Nothing to detract from the wisdom and heritage of the place. The drive through the park was as lovely and peaceful as it must have been a hundred years before. Overlooks, turnouts, and roadside markers, restrained but helpful, appeared every so often along the way. Juniper and ever-present cottonwood lined the Little Missouri, which looped alongside the road in the lowlands. As we drove up an incline to the roundabout circuit, a red-tailed hawk followed us, its sharp eyes on the hunt for unsuspecting lunch. Higher still, a pair of turkey vultures made lazy circles, on the lookout for leftovers.

We parked next to a small stream reminiscent of the sweet splashing of Jakey's Fork where we'd started this journey. While Cherie contemplated the birds hanging out in the riparian scenery, I set off on a promising trail that paralleled the creek. Up a rise and over into a small valley, I found a fat granite boulder, hot and white in the sun. I sat down, pulled off my shoes, and soaked my feet up to my ankles in the icy water. The smell of warming grass, the trickle of the stream, and the light clouds floating overhead invigorated me after long days of driving. I closed my eyes and my mind started to drift …

15

Legacies

Steinbeck said that sometimes people take a trip, sometimes the trip takes them. He added, "Who has not known a journey to be over … before the traveler returns?"

In Teddy Roosevelt's park that day, after many miles on the road and with memories scrolling through my head, I wondered whether it was time to head home. The collection of stories assembled in these chapters (many of which actually happened), the confluences (most of which didn't), and the history (all true, but so much of it sad) could end most anywhere. Why not here, then, sitting beside yet another silvery slip of water as it obeyed gravity's summons to the sea? After all, the course of a river had been a talisman of sorts, leading us out of the Rockies and into the Plains.

I reprised some highlights of our travels through Zane Grey's purple sage.

Jakey's Fork riverine odyssey? Check.

In a marshy meadow at Union Pass high in the Wind River Range of Wyoming, we'd stood next to a freshet small enough to lay a yardstick across. From there, we made our adventurous way downgrade to the flatlands of North Dakota till we reached Bernard DeVoto's Wide Missouri—five football fields across, where it moseyed past Williston, North Dakota.

Confluences? OK, one.

True, we hadn't found these landmarks we'd hoped for, but was I disappointed? Not really. Well, maybe a little. Even old Chris Columbus didn't find exactly what he was looking for. Like the Admiral of the Ocean Seas in reverse, we sailed east to find the west, the historic West. We even found "Indies," in a way, Native Americans Columbus famously misnamed.

Fact and fiction? Both.

We'd shared a bunk with Butch Cassidy. We gaped at vehicular behemoths that slept in campgrounds by night and ate petroleum by day. A couple of days later, we chose not to bed down at a Hitchcockian motel in an eerie town. One town that our map told us about simply wasn't there. It didn't exist. The most recent sleight of hand found us as unwitting tokens plopped down in the virtual world of a computer game. Nearby, quasi-Jurassic beasts sucked oil out of the ground.

The history? Plenty.

The towns and rivers and mountains we'd encountered were kernels of history—signposts, literal and figurative, telling us to stop and look beneath the surface of what we saw. To taste, smell, inhale … to feel the texture of the American West, its achievements and its flaws.

What we name places, whether a mundane Cowboy Café or a Bear Lodge or the indelible Little Bighorn, mark legacies of the West. We'd followed a river that had two names—at one and the same time. There was a chap named Roche eight hundred miles away from his namesake Roche Harbor in the San Juan Islands. We patiently wrote down names like *chwewamink, hechinskayapi,* and *popo agee*; and of course *Tȟatȟáŋka Íyotake* (Sitting Bull), whose tragedy and legacy continue.

The word "legacy" (from the Latin, *ligare,* to bind; think, "ligament") can represent many things, some good: The bequest of a diamond-encrusted pince-nez or admission to a select college because a parent went there. Some, not so good. A legacy can "bind" us to something quite different. The Founders left us the legacy of the Bill of Rights but also ratified a Constitution that endorsed slavery whose virulent strain of racism has not gone away.

An open question, then: Are we bound to continue the legacies of the names we find? What legacies do we bequeath?

At which point, the History Channel promo I was rehearsing in my head got interrupted. A ground squirrel was sitting across the creek next to a burrow and shaking his head. I must have been talking out loud, and he was eavesdropping.

"How about cowboy hats and shiny saddles and country fiddlin' down the street from an espresso shop?" asked the squirrel.

"What about 'em?"

"Window dressing legacies," he spat. "*Your* American West. Haven't you forgotten a couple others?"

"Oh, right. Manuel Lisa."

"Sheesh, get over it," the critter shot back. "No, what about us? Our names. We who live here. Wild. Life."

"Good point. Like bighorn sheep."

"Yep." He pulled out a note pad. "And antelope, grizzlies, black bears, bison, beaver, muskrats, prairie dogs, deer, ducks, eagles, hawks, and geese. The short list."

I pretended to stifle a yawn.

"Or me." He sat up straighter. "Wyoming ground squirrel. *Urocitellus elegans*, to be precise."

Just then, a low shadow came winging toward us out of the creekside trees. The furry morsel-to-be scampered into the underbrush and disappeared. Just as well. Reasoning with smart-ass little rodents was not part of my skill set. But I had to agree about bighorn sheep.

Even though the namesake "spoon horns" themselves were AWOL when we went looking for them, the name of the iconic sheep became shorthand for our trip, mile after many a mile. Beginning in the protected habitat area south of Dubois, the name followed us, and we followed it: The Bighorn River, the Bighorn Basin, Bighorn Mountains, Bighorn National Forest, and a battlefield named after the Little Bighorn. Watersheds, mountains, rivers, valleys, cliffs, and sanctuaries each were legacies of the Rocky Mountains.

I tossed a pebble into the stream to watch the ripples.

A pair of juncos blurted out of the weeds and yipped their annoyance at me. I couldn't blame them. I was getting depressed thinking about the disconnect between restoration of a threatened species today and the legacy of white Americans a century and a half ago who slaughtered the sheep as part of the devastation of the bodies, land, and culture of Native Americans. Then my mind wandered to our seeming birthright, the unremitting search for oil on an ever-warming planet in North Dakota. Before I got started on our Native American "endowment," the birds flew away. It was time for me to go. I hiked back down to the car.

The town of Medora lies just outside the Theodore Roosevelt National Park. Cherie and I talked over whether to continue east or turn back for home. There was a third option. The Roosevelt Expressway continued south into the Badlands of South Dakota and the Black Hills, sacred tribal Sioux territory. Impressive scenery lay that way: The Needles, famously challenging sheer vertical granite spires, tricky State Highway 87's death-defying hairpin turns, and three narrow tunnels through solid rock where a driver is advised to measure the width of his vehicle before entering. But there was an unpleasant taste to the side trip that ruled it out.

True to cartographic arrogance, the destination state park was named after Custer. Worse, the Sioux-named *Hechinskayapi Paha* (Bighorn Mountain; *paha* means "hill") has been renamed "Mount Coolidge." This, the highest point in the state park, was rechristened to commemorate the summer White House of Calvin Coolidge, one of the least worthy of US presidents. A far cry from Teddy Roosevelt, "Silent Cal" longed to escape the heat, bugs, bad air, and people of Washington, DC (his words). Thus, as the `20s roared, he fished for trout while First Lady Grace famously knitted on the front porch.

For the proud sons and daughters of South Dakota, it wasn't enough to steal sacred land and name a park after a disgraced frontier soldier and showman. They went further and persuaded the US Board on Geographic Names to erase a Sioux tribal name of a sacred mountain that had existed for generations, and to rename it after a forgettable president whom H. L Mencken said had a personality like he'd "been weaned on a pickle."

We decided that driving the distance to be further ashamed and angry would be a fool's errand. So, over fresh beverages and a tasty blueberry scone at a coffee shop in Medora, we made our decision. To the west, and home, it would be. We climbed aboard the westbound four-lane high-speed interstate, to brave the "tyranny of the freeway—bumpers and mud flaps," according to one writer. The fewer stops might be a bane and a boon, but surely that was a First World problem. Steinbeck knew the feeling:

> The road became an endless stone ribbon, the
> hills obstructions, the trees green blurs, the
> people simply moving figures with heads but
> no faces. All the food along the way tasted like
> soup, even the soup … The miles rolled under
> me unacknowledged … I know the countryside
> must have been beautiful, but I didn't see it.

That's not how it turned out at all. We stayed a night in Billings, Montana, by the Yellowstone River once again, then continued on Interstate 90, picking up the Clark Fork River on the west side of the Continental Divide. The way felt as fresh as a new travel brochure. With windows down, warm wind whipping by, we'd smile and let a flashy behemoth, a Fleetwood or a Winnebago, overtake us, the four eyeballs inside glued to the fast lane out the front windshield. We gave thumbs up and waves to Phillips 66 or Amoco tankers. Throttle-jockeys rocketed past our pokey 75 mph. In towns, a movie marquee boasted the Butch-and-Sundance flick, a carnival beckoned folks to the rodeo centerpiece, or a four-calendar restaurant called to us, the usual row of pickup trucks parked out front.

In Missoula, we welcomed the Bitterroot River, which joined us from the south. Then came the Coeur d'Alene River, and we followed the pioneers' trail down to the lake where we spent the night. The next morning, I dressed and let myself out of the motel room so as not to awaken Cherie. The day before had been a long haul, and I knew she'd prefer to sleep. But I couldn't. Too much chatter in my brain.

I walked a mile to the Spokane River where it entered the northern lobe of Lake Coeur d'Alene. The streets were quiet in a pre–rush hour on a midweek day in June. The sun sprinkled glitter on the leaves of trees in a riverside park. Diamonds sparkled on wavelets stirred by the breeze. The day would warm up, but it was chilly, and I was glad I'd worn a sweatshirt.

A row of benches faced the river. I sipped slowly on a tasty *café au lait* I'd found at a by-God French *patisserie*. I breathed deeply again and again and finished waking up. Sound from the lake was muffled and soft. Jet Skis and motorboats hadn't started yet. Tourist season hadn't kicked in.

I nodded to a letter carrier making his rounds. A pair of fit young women with matching headbands jogged past, ponytails a-swishin'. An older gentleman walked up and sat on a bench down from me. His dog, an unidentifiable hound, kept busy at the trees and shrubs behind us. The fellow wore a light-gray sport coat, a blue, striped tie, and cordovan leather loafers, but he looked to be Native American—bronze complexion, distinctive nose, dark eyes from what I could see in the morning light.

I imagined he was Nez Perce, a local tribe that had as much tragic history as any, despite being friendly and helpful to Lewis and Clark when they crossed the Rockies into the Oregon Territory. Their Chief Joseph has been immortalized by his final words: "My heart is sick and sad. From where the sun now stands, I will fight no more forever." The once-proud nation's trail of tears, the Nez Perce National Historic Trail, now passes through four states.

I told myself I had to say something to the fellow. Had to, in some minor way, begin to make amends as I'd promised myself I would do. I'd say how sorry I was; tell him how incredibly moved we were when we visited the battlefield. But I caught myself. I'd sound like White Privilege personified. Plus, he'd turn out to be a CPA from Seattle, hand me his card, and say, "What battlefield?"

I kept my mouth shut. I watched the shadows ripple on the river. My seatmate whistled to his pooch, hooked up the leash, rose, and with a nod to me, walked off. But, whoo-ee, that was close. It was definitely time to be home. I walked back through town, looking for a place to grab breakfast and hungry to be back on the road.

Thus, soon we were past Spokane and into the hot-and-dry side of the Evergreen State. US Highway 2 crosses the middle of Washington. In the central foothills of our state, some bighorn herds are "managed" via raffled hunting licenses. We crossed the Columbia at Wenatchee and followed the picturesque river by that name up into the Cascades. There were still patches of snow alongside the road where the highway summited Stevens Pass. From there, the Skykomish River descended to Puget Sound. We made our mandatory stop at Sultan Bakery for doughnuts and coffee, sustenance for the last leg up Interstate 5 to Bellingham— where, for the record, that fall millions of salmon would cruise around in the north Pacific Ocean readying themselves to brave the return up ancestral glacial rivers to spawn. Local Lummis and Nooksacks, Salish tribes in our neck of the woods, net them by the thousands. Sport anglers do their best to compete, and school kids and full-grown adults line the bulkheads and breakwaters to gaze in wonder.

A "confluence" of its own to behold.

Cherie and I are biased, of course. The expanse of the American West always calls to us, its unfettered freedom of movement, distances, history, and time. Living the stories one by one this trip brought us closer to "dim figures of our ever-lengthening past," in the words of Oliver Wendell Holmes. We carry them and their legacies into an uncertain future.

The West itself is a legacy—what has been left to us, what we will leave to those who follow us. There is no denying our insatiable appetite for petroleum or the warming of the planet, desperate herds and flocks of wildlife clinging to existence, nor inexcusable selfishness and bigotry. Some legacies threaten hope. But we cannot unlearn. We cross our fingers and choose Wallace Stegner's wisdom: "One cannot be pessimistic about the West. This is the native home of hope."

His hope might be more tentative today. But what alternative do we have?

16

Postscript
Standing Rock

The sacred Indian Memorial at the Little Bighorn Battlefield, beckoning in peace to the souls of all men killed in war, was the most moving moment of our trip. However, since our return, significant events affecting Native American rights and the oil industry boom in the Dakotas have transpired.

The Standing Rock Sioux Tribe of Indians, joined by other tribes and nontribal, ordinary citizens, in 2016, managed to sidetrack approval by the US Army Corps of Engineers of the North Dakota Access Pipeline, a project by Texas-based Energy Transfer Partners. Corps approval would allow completion of a twelve-hundred-mile pipeline to transport crude oil from North Dakota to Illinois.

The Standing Rock Reservation borders the Missouri River in parts of North and South Dakota. The tribe urged that a rupture or leak in a volatile oil pipeline beneath the river would contaminate groundwater that it had accessed for drinking water for generations. Other environmental issues were raised as a result of a massive, nationwide protest. Though the Corps only had permit authority over the river itself and land adjacent to it that was not part of the reservation, it put a temporary halt to the project.

(Williston and Watford City, which we visited, are well north of the Standing Rock Sioux reservation, do not lie on Indian reservation land, and do not draw water from the Missouri River, which is downstream. Ongoing studies in the Williston Basin where we'd been have thus far turned up no impact on groundwater.)

To wander too far into the thicket of Native American-related case law would be to put at risk both a reader's patience and this writer's expertise. But a brief overview might be helpful. Down the rabbit hole we shall go.

First, the status of Indian tribes. The short, *legal*, answer is that a tribe or nation is considered a separate sovereign entity. The Constitution, ratified in 1788, recognized as much, sort of. "Congress shall have the power to regulate Commerce with foreign nations, and among the several states, and with the Indian Tribes." Article I, Section 8.

As time went on and legal disputes reached the US Supreme Court, previously unforeseen questions arose: Who is subject to taxation or must pay taxes? Who prosecutes crimes, and what does "citizenship" mean? Can tribes print money? Conduct foreign affairs? It must be conceded that when the Constitution was adopted, the fledgling United States had little idea of the extent of indigenous peoples living in the thus-far unexplored western two-thirds of the continent. Lewis and Clark's expedition was still two decades away; the "Northwest" meant the Great Lakes. It probably didn't seem like much of a risk to grant special status to tribes that were more or less "local."

Surely, it was later argued, the Founders could not have meant full sovereignty such as that existing with foreign nations. Yet, even prior to the Constitution, relations with indigenous peoples had been defined in treaties, and treaties are part of the "supreme law of the land." (Article VI, Clause 2.) Shouldn't the rights of Indian tribes be as paramount as those of any sovereign nation?

This overbroad concept clearly would not do. The federal government had a country to run. In an attempt to bridge the gap, tribes came to be defined as "domestic dependent nations"; similar to the relationship of "a ward to its guardian," ruled Chief Justice Marshall in an early decision. (*Cherokee Nation v. Georgia*, 1831.)

Treaties continued to be the operative documents, but with

a catch: one party got to make the rules, decide cases, and enforce the law, often at the end of a rifle. The sad history of treaties made and broken followed. The charade ended with the Indian Appropriations Act of 1871, which declared that in the future there would be no more treaties. Tribes, said the act, were not independent nations after all. As Humpty Dumpty explained to Alice, a word "means just what I choose it to mean, neither more nor less."

A look at the *equitable*—versus strictly legal—issue doesn't pass the straight-face test. Rationalizations over time are laughable. In one shell game, the US government decided it would ensure the "safety and welfare" of otherwise "uncivilized" Native Americans. To Jak end, reservations were established in the most desolate and unusable parts of the West, and whole tribes were banished to them. Treaties were broken on the flimsiest or false pretenses. The story of the "Trail of Tears" and others like it are examples of genocidal cruelty, pure and simple.

Tribal land, if not stolen outright, was broken up into parcels and given to Indians to farm, although they were nomadic hunter/gatherers, not farmers. Land they didn't want would be sold to white settlers. On one day, April 22, 1889, fifty thousand "Sooners" raced to claim two million acres of Oklahoma land unclaimed by neighboring Indian tribes.

Picture a striped cat, sitting in a tree, who disappears, leaving behind only a self-satisfied smile.

Lakota Sioux and other native peoples, including Sitting Bull's Hunkpapas, had roamed throughout the central plains from time immemorial, including in the northwest corner of the Dakotas we visited. The Second Treaty of Fort Laramie (1868) concerned Lakota Sioux sacred land in and near the Black Hills. The invasion of white settlers, in breach of earlier treaties, was among the most egregious. In *United States vs. Sioux Nations of Indians*, the Supreme Court finally ruled *in 1980* that the United

States had wrongfully taken the land under the treaty. Fifteen and a half million dollars was awarded to the tribe. Like Sitting Bull many years earlier who wouldn't accept a pardon (see Chapter 9), the Sioux refused to take the money. It sits in escrow and now amounts to more than one billion dollars.

Tribal sovereignty versus *state* (as opposed to federal) jurisdiction raises a different issue. Since the federal government holds Indian land in trust, a state must defer to federal law. For what it's worth, this general concept has withstood the test of time, but that's not the end of the story. A state, not the federal government, does have the power to determine property law and rights, one of the "reserved powers" under the Tenth Amendment. Here, a student of Constitutional law encounters a conundrum: One line of cases that respects indigenous treaty rights faces off against state cases adjudging individual property rights—rights, for example, of "bona fide purchasers" like you and me. We bought our houses with a clean bill of health from a title company and in accordance with state law. So, too, did schools, churches, governments, and corporations— almost everyone who got a deed. Whose rights should prevail?

    Williston, North Dakota, is not on reservation land. Yet, were a lawyer called upon to advise a client on the subject of his or her or its property rights, he might do well to be careful what he seeks. In my personal experience negotiating on behalf of a local government with a neighboring sovereign nation of Indians, when an impasse was reached over ownership and land use regulation, both parties found it wise to back away from the abyss. In the case of a head-on collision in a court of law, one side inevitably loses—and a precedent is set, possibly binding in future cases and often at an appellate level. A negotiated result is the better solution.

    The Corps of Engineers ruling in the Standing Rock dispute did not depend on who owned what. In fact, no part of reservation land would have been encroached upon by

the proposed pipeline. Nor was the result due to the fact that
the federal government has jurisdiction over transmission
of petroleum, including pipeline safety; nor was it because
shipment of volatile Bakken crude is dangerous and accidents
have cost human lives. Safety regulations, such as they exist,
appear to have been satisfied.

No, the Corps of Engineers chose to rely on another,
superseding federal law. The Environmental Policy Act gives the
federal government authority to require an impact statement
assessing a project's possible injury to the environment. Enough
evidence of potential damage was adduced by opponents to the
pipeline that the Corps finally decided to call for an EIS. Why
wasn't this done in the first place? "It's no use going back to
yesterday," said Alice, "because I was a different person then."

And a different person there is, once again. Within days of
taking office, President Donald Trump flipped the deck and
cancelled the EIS process. Oil now flows through the Dakota
Access Pipeline.

So much for the kaleidoscopic case law in the books, but
this is enough for now.

17

Afterword
The Epigraph

At first blush, the choice of an epigraph from *The Love Song of J. Alfred Prufrock* to introduce a collection of travel stories might seem as unlikely as a preface giving a shout-out to Friedrich Nietzsche. However, the choice of T. S. Eliot's words represents a confluence, including one with a river.

Before decamping to England and going on to well-deserved fame, Eliot, brilliant expat, was born and raised in St. Louis, the self-proclaimed "Gateway to the West" near the conjunction of two great rivers. A posthumous Eliot might profess surprise at a poetic excerpt of his kicking off a series of stories about rivers and exploration of the American West. But that wouldn't be fair. He once wrote, "[The] Missouri and the Mississippi have made a deeper impression on me than any other part of the world."

That said, anyone familiar with *The Love Song* knows that few outlooks on the world could be as far from poor Prufrock's self-puzzling, dystopic, and smoky London and its half-deserted streets than the open expanses and beauty of the American Rockies. In a sense, then, would it not be delightful to see whether poor J. Alfred might get out of his own way and enjoy a road trip like the one we took? On the other hand, Eliot might not have written *Prufrock*, and what a loss that would have been.

Full confession: it also helps that *The Love Song of J. Alfred Prufrock* is one of my all-time favorite poems. It will go with me to the apocryphal desert island if the time comes. I love Eliot's words.

Notes

Some of the sources listed in the Works Cited below require additional comment. They, along with others cited, are among my favorite literary craftsmen, "writers of the purple sage" who have taught me history. Just as often, I've returned to them for the sheer fun of it.

Bernard DeVoto is the patron saint of American West history. His trilogy is indispensable and makes for great reading.

William Goetzmann's *Exploration and Empire* is a definitive, scholarly work that won the Pulitzer Prize in History in 1967.

Cindy Sioux Minkler is a brilliant pianist and an excellent friend who guided me to a source of Hidatsa Sioux language.

A.B. Guthrie's *The Big Sky* and *The Way West* were my first introductions to literature about the opening of the American West. The latter book won a Pulitzer Prize in 1949. Others in Guthrie's Montana "hexology" are *These Thousand Hills, Arfive, The Last Valley,* and *Fuir Land, Fair Land.* Guthrie wrote from his home, his "point of outlook on the universe," Choteau, Montana, on the eastern slope of the Rockies.

Rinker Buck's *The Oregon Trail: A New American Journey* tells of his trip along the historic trail by covered wagon ... in the twenty-first century. I'll say no more.

The entries in the "Montana Trilogy," *English Creek, Dancing at the Rascal Fair, Ride With Me, Mariah Montana* (Barnes & Noble, 1984, 1987, 1990, respectively) are three of Ivan Doig's fiction and non-fiction works, among his many many others. One book in particular, *The House of Sky: Landscapes of the Western Mind* (1977), won a National Book Award.

Timothy Egan's *Lasso the Wind: Away to the New West* (1998) is the tale of a road trip told by the Northwest Corner's favorite New York Times writer.

John McPhee's love of the West, in particular its geology and geography, is unmatched. The two works cited are engrossing, armchair reads. But see also *Encounters with the Archdruid* (1971), conversations with environmentalist and path-breaking Sierra Club director David Brower.

Works Cited

Ambrose, Stephen E. *Undaunted Courage: Meriwether Lewis, Thomas Jefferson and the Opening of the American West*, 1997

de Botton, Alain. *The Art of Travel*, 2004

DeVoto, Bernard. *The Year of Decision: 1846, Across the Wide Missouri, and The Course of Empire*, 1942, 1947, and 1952, respectively.

Campbell, Thomas. *Gertrude of Wyoming*, 1809

Eliot, T. S. *The Love Song of J. Alfred Prufrock*, 1920

Ferris, Timothy. *Life Beyond Earth*, 2000

Gannett, Henry. *The Origin of Certain Place Names in the United States*, 1902

Goetzmann, William H. *Exploration and Empire*, 2000

Heat-Moon, William Least. *Blue Highways*, 1982

Holmes, Oliver Wendell. *The Essential Holmes*, R.A. Posner, *inter alia*. 1992

Matteoni, Norman. *Prairie Man*, 2015

McPhee, John. *Uncommon Carriers, Rising from the Plains, and Basin and Range*, 2006, 1986, 1981, respectively.

McMurtry, Larry. *Lonesome Dove*, 1985

Patchett, Ann. "My Road to Hell Was Paved" in *This Is the Story of a Happy Marriage*, 2013

Redish, Laura. *Native Languages of the Americas*, http://www.native-languages.org/. 2016

Stegner, Wallace. *Marking the Sparrow's Fall: The Making of the American West*. 1999

Steinbeck, John. *Travels With Charley*, 1962

Woolf, Virginia. *Moments of Being: A Collection of Autobiographical Writing*, 1976

Acknowledgments

A heartfelt thanks to my supportive friends in the PenUltimate Writers group, especially Trusted Reader Linda Q. Lambert whose skill and good humor kept this road trip between the white lines. That said, any missed turns, dead-end detours, or wrong-way streets are mine alone.

And of course none of what I write would happen without the patience and love of Cherie, my wife and companion.